The Haunting of Seafield House

By

Caroline Clark

SPOOKY NIGHT BOOKS

Copyright © 2017 Caroline Clark

All Rights Reserved

Caroline Clark

License Notes

This Book is licensed for personal enjoyment only. It may not be resold or given away to others. If you wish to share this book, please purchase an additional copy. If you are reading this book and it was not purchased then, you should purchase your own copy. Your continued respect for author's rights is appreciated.

This story is a work of fiction any resemblance to people is purely coincidence. All places, names, events, businesses, etc. are used in a fictional manner. All characters are from the imagination of the author.

TABLE OF CONTENTS

Prologue	1
Chapter One	7
Chapter Two	27
Chapter Three	37
Chapter Four	47
Chapter Five	55
Chapter Six	67
Chapter Seven	73
Chapter Eight	85
Chapter Nine	97
Chapter Ten	109
Chapter Eleven	119
Chapter Twelve	127
Chapter Thirteen	137
Chapter Fourteen	145
Chapter Fifteen	157
Chapter Sixteen	171
Preview:	189
The Haunting of Brynlee House	189
About the Author	201

Prologue

30th June 1901
Seafield House.
Barton Flats,
Yorkshire.
England.

00:01 am.

Jenny Thornton sucked in a tortured breath and hunkered down behind the curtains. The coarse material seemed to stick to her face, to cling there as if holding her down. Fighting back the thought and the panic it engendered she crouched even lower and tried to stop the shaking of her knees, to still the panting of her breath. It was imperative that she did not breathe too loudly, that she kept quiet and still. If she was to survive with just a beating, then she knew she must hide. Tonight he was worse than she had ever seen him before. Somehow, tonight was different, she could feel it in the air.

Footsteps approached on the landing. They were easy to hear through the door and seemed to mock her as they approached. Each step was like another punch to her stomach, and she could feel them reverberating through her bruises. Why had she not fled the house?

As if in answer, lightening flashed across the sky and lit up the sparsely furnished room. There was nothing between her and the door. A dresser to her right provided no shelter for an adult yet her eyes were drawn to the door on its front. It did not move but stood slightly ajar. Inside, her precious Alice would keep quiet. They had played this game before, and the child knew that she must never come out when Daddy was angry. When he was shouting. Would it be enough to keep her safe? Why had Jenny chosen this room? Before she could think, thunder boomed across the sky and she let out a yelp.

Tears were running down her face, had he heard her? It seemed unlikely that he could hear such a noise over the thunder and yet the footsteps had stopped. *Oh my, he was coming back.* Jenny tried to make herself smaller and to shrink into the thick velvet curtains, but there was nowhere else to go.

If only she had listened to her father, if only she had told him about Alice. For a moment, all was quiet, she could hear the house creak and settle as the storm raged outside. The fire would have burned low, and soon the house would be cold. This was the least of her problems. Maybe she should leave the room and lead Abe away from their daughter. Maybe it was her best choice. Their best choice.

Lightning flashed across the sky and filled the room with shadows. Jenny let out a scream for he was already there. A face like an overstuffed turkey loomed out of the darkness, and a hand grabbed onto her dress. Jenny was hauled off her feet and thrown across the room. Her neck hit the top of the dresser, and she slumped to the floor next to the door. How she wanted to warn Alice to stay quiet, to stay inside but she could not make a sound. There was no pain, no feeling and yet she knew that she was broken. Something had snapped when she hit the cabinet, and somehow she knew it could never be fixed. That it was over for her. In her mind, she prayed that her daughter, the child who had become her daughter, would be safe just before a distended hand reached out and grabbed her around the neck. There was no feeling just a strange burning in her lungs. The fact that she did not fight seemed to make him angrier and she was picked up and thrown again.

As she hit the window, she heard the glass shatter, but she did not feel the impact. Did not feel anything. Suddenly, the realization hit her and she wanted to scream, to wail out the injustice of it but her mouth would not move. Then he was bending over her.

"Beg for your life, woman," Abe Thornton shouted and sprayed her with spittle.

Jenny tried to open her mouth, not to beg for her own life but to beg for that of her daughter's. She wanted to ask him to tell others about the child they had always kept a secret, the one that he had denied. To admit that they had a daughter and maybe to let the child go to her grandparents. Only her mouth would not move, and no sound came from her throat.

She could see the red fury in his eyes, could feel the pressure building up inside of him and yet she could not even blink in defense. This was it, the end, and for a moment, she welcomed the release. Then she thought of Alice, alone in that cupboard for so long. Now, who would visit her, who would look after her? There was no one, and she knew she could never leave her child.

Abe grabbed her by the front of her dress and lifted her high above his head. The anger was like a living beast inside him, and he shook her like she was nothing but a rag doll. Then with a scream of rage, he threw her. This time she saw the curtains flick against her face and then there was nothing but air.

The night was dark, rain streamed down, and she fell with it. Alongside it she fell, tumbling down into the darkness. In her mind she wheeled her arms, in her mind she screamed out the injustice, but she never moved, never made a sound.

Instead, she just plummeted toward the earth.

Lightning flashed just before she hit the ground. It lit up the jagged rocks at the base of the house, lit up the fate that awaited her and then it was dark. Jenny was overwhelmed with fear and panic, but there was no time to react, even if she could. Jenny smashed into the rocks with a hard thump and then a squelch, but she did not feel a thing.

"Alice, I will come back for you," she said in her mind. Then it was dark, it was cold, and there was nothing.

Caroline Clark

Chapter One

25th June 2017
15 Elm Field Road.
London.
England.

2:32 pm.

Gail Parker stopped the car and rested her head against the steering wheel. Suddenly, she felt so exhausted, so totally shattered that she did not think she could walk the few feet back to her house. It was not the walk that she dreaded but having to hide her diagnosis. Having to face Jesse and either tell him what had happened, or even worse, to keep it from him.

Yet now was not the time to give him her news. Jesse was excited, which wasn't unusual. Whenever he found a new house to investigate he was always excited. Only this one seemed different. This time he was so sure, and this time she had agreed to go with him. She would give him this one weekend, and then she would tell him the news. They would face it together, or she would face it alone. It did not matter. Nothing could alter the outcome.

Tears prickled at the back of her eyes but she bit down on her lip and forced them away. A blue Daisy waved at her from the dashboard. When she bought the Volkswagen beetle, the little Daisy had delighted her, yet now she wanted to rip it from the dashboard and stamp on it. A laugh escaped her. As if that would really help.

Pulling down the visor she checked her face. Though her eyes were a little puffy, they were not too bad. This month she had lost 12 lbs, and that hid some of the damage. It didn't look as if she had been crying, she would do.

It was time to put a smile on her face and pretend nothing had happened.

***

Seafield House,
Brinkley Moor,
Yorkshire.

7.45 pm

After a four hour drive, Jesse pulled the 10-year-old Jeep up outside a dilapidated house. The car was his pride and joy, it was the only vehicle that could take all of his equipment. It was not that it was any bigger than other cars, it was just that Jesse had spent years getting it just right, every corner, every nook, and every cranny was filled with custom-made pockets for his equipment. Sometimes Gail would wish he would change it, get something newer, something that had working air conditioning, but she knew it would never happen and the trusty car had never let them down... yet.

Gail was tired, and there was a deep throbbing behind her right eye. All she wanted to do was have a bath, take a couple of tablets and go to sleep. Looking at the rundown place before them, that didn't seem likely.

Jesse was also looking up at the house, she could see the excitement in the set of his jaw, in the way he leaned forward eagerly and slowly scanned the property. Gail bit back the sigh that threatened to escape her and turned her eyes back to the property.

It was almost dusk, the sun was setting behind the house and seemed to bathe it in a dusky rose light. The windows were like mirrors reflecting back at them like empty eyes. It was as if it did not want them to see inside and she felt herself shudder. Quickly, she looked away. It had surprised her that it would be called Seafield House when it was so far from the sea, and yet, now she understood. A field next to the house was filled with long grass. As the wind tickled across its surface, it looked like the ocean. True, a green ocean, but the grass waved and undulated like water. The sight delighted her, and she thought maybe this would not be so bad after all.

Gradually, her eyes were pulled back to the property. It was a large house, dilapidated and obviously empty for many years. Yet surprisingly, there were no broken panes of glass and no graffiti. It was two stories high, the roof had seen better days, and a few tiles had slipped off and laid on the ground below it.

A crumbling wall surrounded the property and between that and the house was dry patchy grass. It looked as if it had been burned by the sun and yet it had not been that hot this year. There were a few trees scattered about. The leaves were bare, their branches just misshapen twigs that reached up to the sky.

The Haunting of Seafield House

For a second, she imagined them beseeching the great god of rain. It was as if they were starved of moisture, starved of something and they were begging for release. Gail shook her head, what was she doing? Jesse was the one who believed in all this and here she was imagining trees begging for water. It looked like she was getting a little carried away.

"I have a good feeling about this place," Jesse said, turning towards her.

Gail nodded. There was a light in his gray eyes and excitement there that had been missing for over a year. This weekend would be good for him, and she would make sure that he enjoyed it as much as he could. Memories might be all they had now, and it was time to create some good ones.

"It's certainly a little creepy," Gail said. "Is somebody meeting us?"

Jesse shook his head and opened the car door. "No, I have the key. Let's get all the equipment inside and then I believe there's a local pub. I don't know about you, but I'm starving. A good meal, and chatting with the locals sounds like the perfect way to get to know the house a little better."

Jesse got out of the Jeep and walked around to the back. He was already unloading equipment as Gail just sat and stared at the house. Something about it disturbed her and yet she knew she was being silly. How many of these houses had Jesse been to? There were dozens, and he had never found a thing. So why was she scared of going into this one? For a moment, tears filled her eyes, she knew it was not the fear of the house but the fear of the unknown to come that made her feel so desolate.

Blinking back the tears, she took one more look at Seafield House. There were six windows on the top floor, and three on either side of the door on the bottom floor. Her eyes were drawn to the uppermost left window, and a gasp escaped her. Just for a moment, she had seen a child, staring from the window. The girl had long dark hair and was wearing a white dress, but then she was gone almost as quickly as she appeared.

"Jesse, look," Gail said and pointed towards the house.

"What is it?" Jesse asked.

Gail found herself staring at the empty window. The glare of the sun made it impossible to see through the glass. What had she seen? As if in answer, a shadow from the clouds passed across the window. Gail laughed.

The Haunting of Seafield House

"I guess I'm just spooking myself, I thought I saw a girl at the window. Good company I'm gonna be."

Jesse had his hand's full of equipment, camera bags over his shoulders. "Don't discount anything you see." he said with a grin. "I want to hear everything no matter how small."

Gail could not help but see the little boy inside the man. Jesse was excited, and part of her hoped that this time he would find something. Another part of her didn't know whether to laugh at such an idea or to be terrified by it. So, she grabbed a couple of bags from the back and followed him into the house.

As she reached the door, Jesse was fumbling with the key. It was large and rusted and looked like something out of a comedy show. Eventually, he had the key ready, juggling with his bags, and she had to stifle another grin. This was typical Jesse, instead of making three trips he piled everything he could hang onto into his arms, over his shoulders, around his neck, and then he'd stumble and shuffle towards the house. Now he had so many bags, and his hands were not free enough to open the door. Gail put her own bags down and took the key from him, giving him a little smile as she did so.

Jesse laughed. "I know, I know. Too many bags, how many times have you told me?"

Despite her headache, Gail gave him a big smile and then turned quickly to the door. How much she loved this man, it hurt her deeply as she thought of his pain to come.

Taking the key in her right hand, she put her left hand on the door. The wood felt rough and crumbly beneath her fingers. As she pushed, it became almost slick and moist as if she had put her fingers into a moldy goo. Every instinct told her to pull back and to run. Maybe she was letting this get to her just a little bit too much? As she tried to insert the key, the door moved away from her. The place was unlocked! For some reason that filled her with dread.

Jesse just laughed. "I guess there's nothing in here to steal so why would it be locked?"

Gail nodded, she supposed that made sense.

Her first view of the house was a little disappointing. It just looked old, dirty and run down. What had she expected?

It took them about half an hour to unpack all of the equipment. They put most of it just inside the door in a large entrance hallway. There were four doors leading off the room and a staircase on the left. Gail watched Jesse check over some of the equipment. She did not know what most of it was. Obviously, she recognized the cameras, the video recording equipment, the tripods, et cetera. Over the years she had heard Jesse talking about much of the rest of it. There were EMF meters, temperature recording equipment, equipment to record radio waves and other waves that she just could not remember. By the time it was all unloaded, she was exhausted and the thought of spending the night in this damp and desolate house filled her with a disquiet that she could not understand. Maybe it was just the idea of being so uncomfortable, of having no electric, no hot water, and the dread of having to tell Jesse about her diagnosis. Yet, something about the place made her hair stand on end.

There were plenty of windows. It should have been light inside, and yet a gloom hung over the place like a heavy cloud. It was also eerily silent, but maybe that was just the difference between a secluded house and living for all her life on a busy London street. There was no traffic noise, no noise from people, and no anything. There wasn't even birdsong or the sound of the wind. The house just seemed quiet. It was almost as if it was waiting for something.

"Are you ready?" Jesse said.

Gail nodded.

Jesse looked more alive than he had in months. There was a constant smile on his face, a spring in his step, and a glistening desire for sheer excitement in his eyes. Watching him made her feel good. It gave her the ability to push away her gloomy thoughts. She would enjoy this night, the excitement of exploring this house together. It was an adventure and one she should relish.

"I'm ready," she said. "How far is this pub and what's it called?"

Jesse laughed a little. "It's only a five-minute walk. It's actually the closest neighbor, being just on the outskirts of the village. Real cheery sounding place. It's called 'The Hanged Man'."

Gail couldn't help but laugh. There was a time when they used to go out for expensive meals, to fancy restaurants, and yet Jesse was more excited about the local village pub with the silly name. Something about his excitement made her feel good.

"Let's go eat," she said and followed him out the door.

This time Jesse did lock up. There was a lot of money's worth in their equipment and more than that, if it was to go missing then the investigation would be a waste of time.

The Haunting of Seafield House

Gail thought back to when she first met Jesse. It had been a Halloween party, in a fake haunted house. She could still remember screaming as she ran around the building with her friends. All of them had had too much to drink, and as the fake skeletons, ghosts, and ghouls had jumped out at them, the shocks had been both frightening and exhilarating. When they made it all the way through the house, there was a big party, and Gail had gone to one side just to catch a breath of fresh air. That was where she met Jesse. They hit it off instantly, and he had told her how he had seen spirits as a child. At the time, she thought he was joking and that it was just a line, but as she got to know him, she knew he really believed it. Apparently, his grandfather had been the same. They believed they could see the souls of those poor individuals who could not cross over. Yet, when Jesse hit puberty, he stopped seeing ghosts, and he had always sought to relive those times or to find an explanation for what he saw. He was driven to know if he had really seen those things, or if it was merely the imaginings of a child driven by stories from an elderly relation.

Gail really hoped that this house would give him answers. At 24, Jesse was in the final year of a degree in paranormal studies. When he had first chosen the degree, they had argued about it for weeks. Gail was in many ways the exact opposite of Jesse. She only believed in what she could see, touch, and measure. Maybe that was why she became an architect. It was a good job and one she really loved. Most of the time she was simply designing houses for a building company, but every now and then she got to do something really exciting. Maybe she should look at this house as a project. If there were strange goings on here, maybe they could be explained by the build of the house. It was a comforting thought.

Jesse took her hand in his, and they started to walk down the path and away from the house. As they stepped onto the streets, Gail felt as if a weight was lifted from her shoulders. She turned back to look at the house, and a shiver ran down her spine.

"You feel it too, don't you?" Jesse said with a big grin on his face.

Before she could stop herself, Gail nodded, and she watched as his grin widened.

"I knew it," he said. "This is the place, this is where my questions are answered, and my work is validated. I cannot thank you enough for coming with me. This is gonna be great, Gail, just you wait and see."

Gail nodded. How she hoped that he would find answers. That he would find something to keep him going through the long months ahead, and yet her stomach twisted inside of her and she suddenly felt a little sick.

The Haunting of Seafield House

***

The walk to the pub took only five minutes as Jesse had said. It was the first building in the small village of Brinkley Moor and was a pretty little pub. It was a typical Tudor building built of wood, wattle, and daub. It had been well maintained, and the walls outside were festooned with baskets of trailing petunias. The deep purple and bright white of the flowers brought a smile to her face.

Outside the pub were a number of tables and at least three of them were occupied. One with a courting couple and the other two with families. The sounds of the children laughing and talking brought a pang to her heart and once again her eyes were filling with tears. *She would never have children.*

The pub sign caught her eye. Though she had not known what to expect she did not expect something quite as graphic. The dark and dreary house showing a hanged man could have been Seafield. The hanged man in question had bulging red eyes and a thick and swollen tongue dangling from his mouth.

"What a strange sign," she said without even thinking.

Jesse laughed. "It's not the first time I've seen it. Note the resemblance to Seafield House. It looks like the landlord will be dealing in rumors. This could be good. I could get some really great information about the property's past."

Jesse led the way into the pub. It was nice and old worldly inside except for the addition of spotlights. These seemed to be everywhere in the ceiling, shining down on the tables that gave the place a light and airy feel, and yet they hurt Gail's eyes. One of the first symptoms she had noticed was a sensitivity to light. Maybe if she had sought help, then things could have been different... Only that road was not one she would go down. It was too late to play the 'what if' game.

It wasn't until the headaches had become unbearable that she had gone to her doctor's and been given the terrible news. The sound of Jesse talking to the barman brought her out of her melancholy.

"Do you want a drink before we eat?" Jesse asked with a big smile on his face.

Gail nodded.

"White Zinfandel?" Jesse asked.

Gail nodded again, maybe the wine would relax her, maybe it would mix with the tablet she was taking and, at least for a short while, the pain would be gone.

The Haunting of Seafield House

While Gail looked at the menu, Jesse spoke to the landlord. His name was Ben, and he was a big man with a wide-open smile and a thick mop of dark hair that was just touched with gray at the temples. He seemed more than happy to tell them about the house.

Jesse had already ordered a curry. At times, she wondered if he ate anything else, but tonight she could not face anything hot, and so she ordered scampi and chips. While they waited for the order, Jesse listened to Ben talk about the house. It was good to see, his eyes were bright, his smile ready. It was as if he was taking in everything, feeding off it and sifting the information. She knew he was no fool, that he could work out what was fake and what could be real and it was really good to see him so happy in his work.

"No one spends a night in that house, that I guarantee you," Ben said with a smile that clearly told her he had heard it all before.

"This is not my first rodeo," Jesse said. "I have thousands of pound's worth of highly calibrated equipment. Not only will it tell me if something is there. It will tell me where they are, what they are, and what they are doing. If this house is anything other than a hoax, then I will find it, and I will prove it."

"You're not the first to say that," Ben said before he took Jesse's glass and pulled him another pint. "We have had them all, and every one of them has left that house in a hurry, most have left it screaming. I've even heard tell that some of them never recovered. You really wanna put your little lady through all that?" Then he gave a big grin and a wink in Gail's direction.

Normally, she would have been annoyed with such behavior, but there was something about Ben that didn't insult. It wasn't meant in a bad or demeaning way, in fact, he was even including her in the conversation and still the warning he gave worried her more than she could say.

"Well, I've heard all this talk about spooky goings on in the night," Jesse said, "how about giving me some real information. What happened at the house?"

Ben stepped back from the bar, picked up a glass and polished it on the cloth he had in his hands. Maybe this was just showmanship, maybe he had done it a thousand times, and yet there was something about his reactions. It was as if he was nervous to say too much.

"While there have been various stories throughout the years," Ben said. "No one stays there the full night. No matter how many try, none of them have ever lasted all night. All you Ghost Hunters, you come down here every so often and every one of you thinks they are the

The Haunting of Seafield House

one that will uncover the secret. I can tell you this for nothing, I would never go into that place no matter what. No amount of money would get me across the threshold."

Jesse started to laugh. "Heard it all before, Ben. Tell me something specific, something I don't already know."

Ben seemed to think for a moment, and then he let out a long sigh. "All right, I'll tell you.

"They say the original ghost was a woman, Jenny Thornton, murdered by her husband, Abe. The story goes that he threw her from a window and that before she died, she promised that she would come back and that he would never rest."

"That's the story I've researched," Jesse said. "Some tales talk about a daughter, only the details are sketchy. It's as if the daughter existed and yet didn't exist and some tales say it's a daughter that is the ghost. So, if that's all you've got, Ben, then you ain't scaring me."

Ben chuckled and carried on polishing his glasses. "I have more... you see, a lot more has happened in that house than just that tale. The next major incident was in 1969. The house had been sold and left and sold and left time and time again before that, but no one ever stayed more than a week. The couple who moved in in 1969, some say they had a daughter, some say they were on their own. It was the night of the moon landing that it happened... everyone that had one was watching telly. Apparently, the neighbors heard screaming. When the police got there, the husband had stabbed his wife, time and time again. It is said he was in a frenzy and stabbed her over thirty times. When the coppers found him, he was really calm, handed himself in and stood staring at the house while they were dealing with her. All the time the officers swore they could hear a child crying and they saw a child at the window. Yet, after the woman's body had been taken away, the man said they had no children, and that no children were in the house. To be sure, the police searched the house but they never found a child."

"Domestic violence cases might spark a ghost but there again, it might just be another drunk husband." Jesse took another drink of his pint and gave Ben a challenging look.

Ben nodded, his whole face said he was up to the challenge. "It seemed that while the police were searching the house, the husband somehow got away. Next thing they know he was up at the window, the far left window as you are looking at the front of the house."

Gail felt herself shudder, that was the window that she thought she saw a child.

"Two officers swore they saw a child or a small woman pushing him from that window. They searched for that person, for that child, for that woman... no one was ever found. It was ruled that he jumped from the window and died, that it was a suicide."

"Are there records on this?" Jesse asked.

Ben nodded. "It will all be in the local archives. Following that incident, there have been over a dozen unexplained deaths, five suicides from that same window. People walking past hear a child laughing, they see a child in that window, and yet, no local children will go near that place. You make of that what you will, but I warn you... do not go back there. Don't even go back for your equipment, spend the night here if you wish, no charge and then drive home and stay safe."

"Very funny," Jesse said.

"You know the legend." Ben looked from Jesse to Gail and she felt her stomach turn. She didn't know the legend.

"Stay after dark and you will never leave," Jesse said and laughed. "It's the same with all these houses.

"No," Ben said. "It's not. I have seen people go in that house over the years and any who stayed after dark… they were never there in the morning. Do me a favor, don't go back there."

Jesse laughed but Gail could not help but feel uncomfortable.

Ben turned away to serve another customer, Gail wanted to agree with him. Suddenly, the last thing she wanted to do was to go back to that house. The thought of spending the night there all in the dark set her nerves on edge. There was one thing she really hated more than anything, and that was the dark. Yet, as she turned to Jesse, she could see the excitement bubbling inside of him. He was like a hound that had caught the scent of blood, and there was no way he was giving up the trail.

Chapter Two

They spent just an hour in the pub, eating at the bar, while Jesse questioned Ben over more details about the house. At first, it had all been jovial, but as the night wore on, she could see that Ben was getting more nervous. It was as if he was buying into his own tale, and yet Jesse just seemed more excited.

"It's been really good to talk to you," Jesse said as they got ready to leave.

Ben nodded and then he looked right at Gail. "Why don't you stay here the night?" he asked. The lines around his eyes seemed deeper giving him a weary look that worried her just a little. "You look a little unwell, and maybe a hot bath and a nice comfortable bed would be much better than sleeping in a drafty old house."

"Steady on," Jesse said. "We're a team, and she's safer with me than here."

His eyes were mocking, but Gail could sense a touch of jealousy. Though she really wanted that bath, she knew that it would let Jesse down badly. So she shook her head. "Thanks, but I really am looking forward to this."

Ben picked up another glass and absently polished it. "Okay, well, you kids keep safe, and if things go wrong, you are welcome here anytime."

Jesse laughed and, putting his arm around Gail, he thanked Ben and steered her from the pub.

The night air was cooler but still pleasant, and there was a full moon in the sky. It made the walk back to the house enjoyable. Jesse had his arm around her shoulder, and Gail was leaning against him just a little. It felt so good, and she wanted to just curl up in his arms and forget everything. Maybe tonight would be exciting. A little like camping and they could have some good times.

Everything felt fine until they walked through the gate and back onto the property. Almost immediately she was colder, and the air was somehow heavier. It was a strange kind of pressure that made her feel down, depressed, bringing back her headache and she could not explain it. Unless, of course, she was just feeling anxious and her own anxiety was making her feel this way?

Jesse unlocked the door and then pushed. It opened a crack and then slammed back. To Gail, it looked as if someone was pushing but Jesse ignored it and just leaned harder on the door. It opened easily this time, and he led her back into the house. It was dark and creepy, but he had some LED lamps that he set up in the small room just off the entrance hall.

"This is where we will spend the night," he said as he looked around. "It feels like a solid room and we can still see out into the house and can set the equipment up in the entrance with cameras in each room.

Gail looked at the floor, it was dusty, dirty and there were small footprints clearly showing. "What are these?" she asked.

"Looks like Ben was wrong and the local kids do come in here."

"Oh," was all that Gail could manage.

"Spirits don't leave footprints," Jesse said. Then he reached over and took her hand. "They don't push people out of windows either. Don't let Ben's tall tales get to you. Some very desperate spirits can move small objects, but they can't push you from a window or cause you harm. Trust me, you are safe here."

Gail sighed and leaned against his chest. It felt so good to feel his muscles and warm body. It was solid and real, and he smelt of musk and the subtle aftershave he used. Gently, he put his arms around her for a few moments, and she wanted to stay there all night, but she could tell he was eager to be getting on. So, she pulled back and reached up and pecked him on the lips.

"Get the equipment ready, I will set up the sleeping bags and then we can have a look around."

Ben nodded and left the room with one lantern. As he walked out, the swinging of the lamp cast crazy shadows across the walls. It was as if something was floating above her and it set her heart pounding. Then the light was gone, and the room plunged into dusk. With just the one lamp, the light barely reached the corners. Gail shuddered as the darkness seemed to reach out towards her. Shaking the feelings away she pulled out their camping mats and cleared an area of the floor near the far wall. First, she lay down the mats and put the sleeping bags on top. Then she set up the small stove and fetched the water and things for a drink. It was their nighttime routine to always have a drink of either wine or hot chocolate before bed.

Just as she had finished, Jesse came back in holding a meter in his hands. It was buzzing, and he had a huge grin on his face.

"What is it?" she asked.

"We have EMF!"

As the meter buzzed, Gail felt as if the pressure was building up outside her head. It felt as if tiny hands were pressing on her skull and crushing her brain. She wanted to shout, to tell it to stop but she knew it was just her illness and that she just had to breathe through it.

"What now?" Gail asked.

"Follow me and let's see if we can find us some spirits." Jesse left the room grinning like a child on Christmas morning.

Gail followed him out into the hallway. It was darker here. There was one small lantern that he had put at the far end of the hall. Shadows coalesced around the corners of the room, and the light hardly penetrated more than a few feet. Gail knew the stairs were to their left. They looked worn and old, and she wondered if they would hold their weight. Maybe there was more danger here than just ghosts?

Cold air lifted her hair and tickled across her neck, she turned quickly, but there was nothing there. "Jesse?"

"It's just a breeze," he said as if reading her thoughts. Moving forward the light he was carrying went with him, and the darkness swarmed all around her.

"There are tiles missing, gaps in the windows and doors. You will feel all sorts of air that will not be spirits," Jesse said as he walked across the room. "Don't worry, I will let you know if we have any actual activity."

Gail nodded even though she realized he couldn't see her. Catching up with him she followed his route across the hallway. She could see that he had cameras and sensors set up all around. Some of them had red lights blinking, another machine sent a blue beam across the room, backward and forward. It reminded her of something out of a sci-fi film and for some reason she didn't want to touch the beam.

Jesse was wearing a small head torch with an inbuilt camera. All the cameras were feeding back to a laptop in the other room. Later, they could monitor from there, and she could not wait. Walking about no longer seemed fun. The head torch's beam was deliberately made narrow and provided little light as Jesse pointed the meter around the room. The buzzing changed depending on the direction, and he began to walk away from the equipment, away from her.

Gail felt her stomach clench, and goose bumps rose on her arms. "Should I bring a lantern?" The last thing she wanted was to be alone in this place. It just did not feel right. Maybe it was the draft, the fear of the roof falling in or maybe it was the small footprints in the dust when Ben had said no one came in the house.

"No, the darker, the better, we don't want to cause too much disruption."

You speak for yourself, Gail thought.

Jesse was walking towards the first of the doors, and she rushed to catch up. The small beam of his torch cast across its surface. Dirty, once cream paint was flaking and peeling off the wood. As the beam moved across the door, she saw deep scratches. Jesse reached down and turned the handle. It was one of the old, round type handles and though it was green with age, she thought it had originally been brass.

The door moved away from them with a creak, and for a minute she wanted to laugh. That had been so typical of a low budget horror film that it broke the fear and made her realize that this was just an old house. Suddenly, she was looking at it with different eyes. It could be a nice property, it could be renovated and brought back to use. They stepped through the door and Jesse had to duck a little. Typical of the age of the property the doors were not too big.

The wind whistled past them causing her heart to pound as she jumped back. *Stop this,* she admonished herself. There would be a logical answer. Putting her mind into architect mode, she looked around the room. Sure enough, there was a pane missing from one of the windows.

There was very little in the room. Just a few bits of furniture, which looked old and possibly valuable. Why had the place not been looted? It made little sense. Most houses of this age, if they were left empty, would have been stripped. Someone would have surely come and emptied this property, whether with the owner's permission, or more likely, late one night.

"There's nothing here," Jesse said, and he pushed a camera into the wall before turning and walking out of the room.

"Good, can we leave?" Gail said the words before she even thought and Jesse turned to look at her.

The head torch was shining directly in her eyes, and it seared through her delicate retina's and right into her damaged brain. Blinking rapidly she raised a hand and gasped.

Jesse moved the torch to one side. "Sorry, are you all right?"

Gail bit back the tears and fought against the pain. Could she have any more painkillers yet?

"Gail, are you all right?" Jesse asked again.

"It's just a headache," she said. "I will be fine."

"Are you sure?"

Gail nodded and forced a smile on her face. So much for supporting him this weekend.

Jesse reached out and took her arm. "Good, when I said nothing here I meant in this room. There is definitely something in this house."

"A ghost?" she asked wondering if she really wanted to know.

"That's not certain yet. It could be power lines, old mine shafts, or even a hoax but I can feel a presence here, maybe I'm wrong, but this is the most I've felt since I was thirteen. I can't thank you enough for coming with me, for supporting me." Gently, he took her hands in one of his and squeezed. A buzzing sound had Gail jumping backward. Jesse laughed, and the meter kept picking up something. He waved the meter at her.

"What?" Gail asked.

"I don't know," Jesse said. "That's what's so exciting."

Chapter Three

Jesse turned away from her. All he could see was the meter, and he waved it from side to side. Gail had heard it buzz, had seen the needle spike. As it did, she felt the pressure increase. It was as if the air was being sucked from the room. Watching Jesse, she knew she should be excited. This was what he had wanted for so long, but she could not feel anything but dread.

"This way," he said and walked along the edges of the room.

Gail followed him feeling her sense of dread grow with each footstep. The boards of the floor creaked, the meter buzzed and she could hear a ringing in her ears. The latter was probably not relevant, but it only increased her anxiety. As they skirted the hallway, the dark seemed to press down all around. In her mind, it was a living thing that wanted to reach out and suffocate them. It wanted nothing more than to snuff out their lives and its inky dark finger seemed to grasp into the narrow focus of light.

Jesse led the way. He stopped.

BANG!

Gail jumped backward, her heart in her throat, her head pounding. What was wrong with her? She knew what had happened, he had simply tapped on the wall. Looking for hollow spots, for damage, for anything that could explain the EMF.

Jesse continued on around the room, they passed in front of the lamp, and as they got closer to it, Gail felt better. It was as if the light was a place of refuge and she wanted to stay within the sanctuary of its glow. Only Jesse was moving on so quickly. He opened another door. This one looked in better condition, and it opened smoothly and silently. Gail caught up and looked over his shoulder. The room was empty save for an old chair and some scattered sheets of faded newspaper. Jesse moved his head left to right, and the thin beam splayed across the room, but there was nothing to see. Walking in, his feet crunched on the paper, and Gail looked down. It was the local weekly and as she stared at the scattered and faded sheets her breath caught in her throat. Each sheet told a story of the house. Of a suicide or a murder and they were spread across the decades. Over fifteen different faces looked up at her, and their eyes seemed to be pleading.

"What!" she said, but Jesse was still walking. Slowly, he skirted around the room while Gail was rooted to the spot, but the light moved with him. It was surreal, just this tiny beam of hope in the blackness but she could not move. No matter how she tried, she could not risk standing on those faces. Holding her breath, she hunkered her shoulders down and tried to be as small and insignificant as she could be. Tried to pull in her arms in case there was something there, something reaching out for her but nothing came. Her lungs burned desperate for air, but she could not breathe.

Then Jesse had completed his circuit of the room, and he was back at her side. "Nothing in here," he said, and the disappointment was clear in his voice. Once again he pushed a camera into the wall and left it there sending its signal back to the laptop.

"But... but the papers," Gail said.

Jesse pointed his head down at the floor, and Gail let out a gasp. All she saw was old and faded newspapers, there were no photos, just lots of print too faded and damaged to read.

"I..." she could not finish.

"Did you see something?" he asked.

Gail did not know what to say. She had been told that her illness, her brain tumor would make her see things. How did she know if what she saw was real? "I... I don't know," she said.

Jesse stuck the now quiet meter in his pocket and took her hands. "I know this is scary for you," he said. "But you must trust me. If you see things, then let me know. Anything could be important, it could make all the difference to my investigation."

For a moment Gail thought about lying, but he was right, maybe it was her imagination, maybe it was a hallucination brought on by a temporal lobe tumor, or maybe it was what he was looking for. "I thought I saw faces on the newspaper sheets. Faces of people who had died in this house. Just for a moment, they seemed to be pleading with me."

Jesse let go of her hands. "Really!?" he asked.

Was he hurt? Was he upset that she had felt something and he hadn't? Then she understood that he would be. This was his life. As a child, he had seen spirits, had spoken to them along with his grandfather. Then when he hit puberty, his grandfather died, and his gift left him. All these years he had been looking to get it back, and now it was her who felt something. How could she be so insensitive?

"I think maybe it's just my imagination and all the spooky tales from the pub," she said weakly.

Jesse's face cleared and he gave her a smile. "Maybe, but who knows. Don't worry about my feelings, if you see or feel something let me know. Okay?"

Gail nodded and followed him back into the hallway.

There was only one door left, one room left and then they would have to go up the stairs. For some reason, that thought turned her blood to ice and set her knees a shaking.

Jesse walked on and came to the last door. It was closest to the lamp he had hung, and it felt good to walk into the light. Maybe it was just her mind playing tricks, but it felt safer somehow. Yet, as he got to the door the meter buzzed and the air turned colder. Jesse turned to her, a smile on his lips as he flashed the headlamp across her face. Gail screwed up her eyes and bit down on her lip to control the pain, but she smiled back her encouragement.

Jesse tried the door, but it would not budge. "It must have gotten damp and swollen," he said, and he leaned his shoulder against it and shoved hard. Still nothing. Jesse handed her the meter and stepped back. The meter seemed to vibrate in her hands as it buzzed and the needle hit the red at the top. What should she do? Before she could ask Jesse kicked the door and it opened a little too easily and he was pitched forward and out of her view.

As Jesse disappeared, the meter in her hand let out a shriek. The needle hit the red and seemed to bounce and shake at the top of its scale. Gail almost dropped it as her heart leaped into her mouth and her stomach plummeted. It was cold, so very cold, and her breath streamed out before her. Had something taken Jesse, it seemed so silly so unbelievable, and yet suddenly she felt chilled to the bone. At that moment she did not know what to do. Should she run into the room after him, or run to the pub and ask them for help? A lump formed in her throat, goosebumps rose on her arms, and for long seconds she could not even move. Despite the cold, the air felt heavy, oppressive. It seemed to press down on her forcing her to the ground.

The sound of laughter broke her spell, and she stepped into the room.

"Jesse, Jesse, where are you?" she called into the darkness.

A shadow loomed towards her, and she let out a shriek and raised her hand to fend it off.

"Easy there, easy," Jesse said. "It's only me."

As he said the words, everything came into view. It had simply been the shadow from the head torch creating a diaphanous monster.

"What happened?" she asked, putting a hand on her chest to try and calm her racing heart.

Jesse came to stand beside her and turned so that his light illuminated some of the room. It was a kitchen, old-fashioned, dirty, and littered with newspaper.

"I guess the door just gave way," Jesse said. "I tumbled in, practically did a forward roll before landing on my back in a most ungraceful manner."

Gail could not help but laugh at the picture he described. Maybe they could have some fun tonight. Maybe she was just being silly and letting her imagination run away with her. After all, when had she ever believed in ghosts?

"Did I hear the EMF meter spiking?" Jesse asked.

Gail remembered the squeal and the way the needle had hit the red on the meter. It did not make her feel quite as confident to think that the equipment had registered something at the same time as she had felt... what had she felt? Maybe it had been nothing. Just a strange feeling which was understandable considering Jesse had disappeared through a door. So it had been cold, that didn't mean anything.

"It squealed, just as you fell through the door," Gail said. "Unless that was you?" She could not help but let out a laugh.

Jesse gave her a mock hurt expression and laughed too.

"I told you we would have some fun," he said and took the gauge from her.

At the moment it looked dead and registered nothing at all. Jesse twiddled with the buttons, held it to his ear, and then twiddled again. A look of disappointment came over his face.

"I think we are getting close," he said. "Maybe there's a basement. If so, it will probably be from this room. The kitchen. I couldn't find any plans for the house. Though I did find many mentions of a search for bodies.

The usual place for such a search is the basement or the garden. Yet, many times such searches have taken place and the spirits hide their remains until the right person comes along. Until someone persuades them, it is time to let go. Come on, I have a really good feeling about this."

Caroline Clark

Chapter Four

The kitchen was very basic. Jesse set up a bigger camera this time as Gail looked around the room. There was one window over the sink and a door to the outside. The glass in both were smeared and dirty, and it was impossible to see through them. As they walked into the room, a cobweb filament tickled straight across Gail's face, and her hands flew up to tear it away. One thing she had always hated was spiders. All those legs and the beady eyes just gave her the creeps. Then, of course, there was the fact that her father used to tell her not to sleep with her mouth open. For if she did, a spider would make its nest there. Even now, just the thought of it made her shudder.

Dilapidated old units covered one wall of the kitchen. Some of the doors were hanging off, and paint was peeling from the others.

There was an old ceramic sink. It looked like the tap had been leaking and a red-brown stain ran down one side and all across the bottom. It glistened in the light from the head torch. Something about it turned her stomach, there was a slight coppery stench, and Gail imagined if she touched it that it would be slick and moist. Somehow, it reminded her of blood only that was stupid. It was just an old rust stain.

Jesse moved on around the kitchen, the meter held in front of him, the head torch casting shadows across the room that seemed to make her jump. He knocked on the walls, opened cupboard doors, and took his time looking at everything. There was a faint buzzing from the EMF meter, and she could hear Jesse as his breathing became more rapid. He thought they were onto something.

Gail wanted to ask if they could leave. Yet she knew it was not the right time. As they walked across the kitchen, they saw a small table with four chairs stacked around it. It was old and poor quality. In fact, it looked as if it would hardly hold any weight and was almost about to collapse in front of them. The EMF raised up another notch, and the noise got faster as well as higher in pitch. It sounded like a warning, like some angry bird alerting the flock to danger and yet Jesse did not seem to notice. In fact, his breathing increased even more, and he hurried on around the kitchen. As he waved the meter from side to side, the head torch followed. Gail tried to see as much as she could, but the shadows and jumping light were making her headache worse by the minute. For a second, she closed her eyes and pressed her hand to her temples. As she opened them, she noticed footprints in the dust on the floor. They were small and very well defined, and were made by the bare feet of a child or a very small adult. A gasp escaped her.

Who had been here?

"Jesse, do you see these?" she asked.

He let out a sigh, and she knew he wanted her to be quiet, but this was too important.

"The footsteps," she said. "They lead that way." Gail pointed in the darkness and felt a little silly until Jesse turned towards her. The light shone right in her eyes, and the pain was so intense that she almost dropped to her knees. Squeezing her eyes tightly shut she fought down a wave of nausea and felt herself sway.

A hand reached out to steady her.

"Gail, Gail, are you all right?" Jesse's voice was full of concern as his arm held her steady.

"It's just a headache," she said. "I'll be okay."

"Maybe I should take you to the pub. You could spend the night there."

A big part of Gail wanted to say yes. To jump at the chance, but there was another part of her that did not want to leave him alone, not in this house and yet she could not understand why. This was not the first time he had been in situations like this. Jesse was not frightened, if anything, he was excited. So, why didn't she leave, why didn't she let him take her to somewhere warm, comfortable, and safe? As she thought about it, she knew why. Gail did not believe he was safe and for some reason, she thought it would be worse if she was not there.

"No, no, I'm okay. I want to stay here with you. This is more fun than I thought and I will be all right." Gail put on a smile as best she could and hoped the words sounded more genuine to Jesse than they had to her.

For a moment he stared at her, and she thought he would say more. That maybe he would insist on her leaving. Instead, he shook his head and smiled.

"As long as you are sure. If you get too bad just let me know. It's only a quick drive down to the pub, and I will be fine here all alone."

"Thanks, but I think I will be fine. The footsteps," she said and pointed to the floor.

Jesse lowered the lamp and pointed in the direction of her finger. Sure enough, the small, almost perfectly defined footsteps led across the dusty floor. She could see the excitement in Jesse's eyes before he turned to follow them. They led away from the table, towards the opposite wall. Gail followed him, and as she did, she felt a cold breeze across her back. The hair raised on her neck and she leaped forward as a crash sounded behind her. Jesse spun around and put himself in front of her. Gail was cringing, waiting for what, she did not know, but nothing happened, and she peeked out from behind his shoulder. One of the kitchen chairs had fallen over and lay in pieces on the floor.

"Did you do that?" Jesse asked.

"No, I wasn't anywhere near it."

"Are you sure?"

For just a moment Gail doubted herself, had she caught it? Only that didn't make sense; surely, she would have felt it if she had.

"Yes, I'm sure, I was just behind you."

Jesse reached down and picked up a piece of the wood from the chair it was rotten and crumbling.

"Maybe it just collapsed?" he stated, and as he turned back the EMF meter shrieked a little louder.

Jesse waved his arm in front of him left to right and as he did the shrieking rose and lowered. Eventually, he found the highest point and headed in the direction of the footsteps.

Gail followed, and yet her feet felt like lead, and every step was exhausting.

Every few paces the EMF got louder, and Jesse moved a little quicker. Soon they had covered the room and were stood in front of a wall. Even from the poor light of the head torch, Gail could see that the footsteps ended in front of the wall. It was as if the child had walked through it.

"What now?" she asked.

Jesse was running his hands across the wall.

"There has to be something here," he said. "So, we find it."

Now he was tapping on the wall. Tap tap tap, tap tap tap, tap tap thud. The noise changed, and she could see the excitement on his face.

"What does it mean?" Gail asked even though she already knew. As an architect, she understood that the sound signified a hollow space. It was possible that it was loose paneling, but she doubted that. There was probably a hidden room and yet she really hoped she was wrong.

"This could be the entrance to the cellar," Jesse said. "If I can find a way in I think we are onto something."

He passed over the EMF to Gail. It felt strange in her hand as it shrieked out a warning. The needle was going into the red almost all the time and each time it did she felt a shock course through her. It was only nerves, but it felt real. While she stood there holding the meter as far away from her as she could, Jesse tapped and searched the wall. Now she could see it clearer she could see that it was covered in wood panels. After some time he found a loose one and pulled it free. There was a blank space behind it. Jesse turned and grinned at her.

"We found it," he said and then carried on pulling off planks before she had time to stop him.

Caroline Clark

Chapter Five

Soon enough all the planks had been removed to reveal a dark opening. It had obviously once been a doorway and stone steps led down into the depths below. Jesse turned towards her and gave her a great big smile. As he did the light flashed across her face and the pain flared inside her head. He was getting better, and the glare only stayed there for a moment, so she bit down on her lip, a taste of blood filling her mouth, and she swallowed it down as she looked into his big gray eyes. They were filled with excitement, with passion, and were the most alive she had seen them in over two years. Jesse needed this, and as much as the thought of going into that cellar terrified her, she knew that she would go.

"Maybe we should get a bigger lamp?" Gail asked.

"The dark can't hurt us," Jesse said. "Yet, it is better for the infrared camera on my head, and it is better for any spirits that may be left here. If they have been alone for some time, they will be scared. Too much light is difficult for them. So, it's always best if we keep it to the minimum."

Gail guessed she understood what he was saying but knew she would feel better with a bigger lamp. Still, Jesse knew what he was doing more than she did and the more light there was, the more her head pounded, so she accepted his expertise.

"When are we going down?" Gail asked, and yet she knew the answer already.

"There's no time like the present," Jesse said with a wink.

Taking the EMF from her, he turned towards the dark hole and let the light chase down into its depths. It was covered in cobwebs, and dusty paint was flaking from walls. The stone steps looked worn and uneven. As she got nearer, she could feel a stream of cool damp air rising from below. A musty odor, a little like rotting meat, filled her nostrils. The smell clogged at the back of her throat and made it hard to breathe and for a moment she thought that she would be sick.

Jesse didn't notice, he was stood on the threshold ready to step down into whatever lay below.

"What happens when we get down there?" Gail asked.

"We look around, take more footage on the headcam, take some readings and see if we can find anything. Maybe we can find remains or even the spirit. If we do, then we work out why it's here, and we document it as well as we can. Isn't this just the most exciting experience you've ever had?"

Gail tried to put on a smile, but it never reached her eyes. It didn't matter, Jesse was so excited he was already stepping down into the darkness below.

Each step down into the cellar filled Gail with terror. Not only was she constantly covered in cobwebs, the thought of the spiders was almost more than she could bear. There was also the stench from below and the cold air brushing past them... but more than anything it was the darkness. The head torch barely penetrated more than a few feet in front of Jesse, and she had to rush to keep up with him. To stay close to the bubble of light.

The excitement in him was obvious. This was a dream come true, an accumulation of years of searching, of researching and it was a validation of his past. A validation of his grandfather. Even though it was hard for her, Gail knew it was worth it, so she gritted her teeth, her arms flapping like a windmill against the cobwebs as she followed him down into the cellar.

It seemed to take forever and yet there were only 15 steps. Gail knew this because she counted every last one. The floor felt like dirt beneath her feet. She had expected it to be hard packed and yet it was loose and powdery, and it was so quiet and still down here, that it felt like they were in a vacuum.

Jesse stepped into the cellar and slowly started to walk around it. The EMF had gone quiet. She did not know if he had turned it off or if it no longer picked anything up. It seemed strange if it was the latter. To Gail, the cellar felt crowded. It was as if they were not alone, she could almost hear people whispering, and was expecting their hands to touch her back, and yet there was nobody there. It was like a pressure, a presence, something just out of the corner of her eye. How could Jesse cope? It seemed to be building and Gail wanted to scream and yet he was so calm before her.

Jesse walked slowly in front of her and did not acknowledge anything was wrong.

Did he feel it?

Was it just her?

Was it just her tumor making her see things that were not there?

Slowly, he checked the room searching the floor for any signs of disturbance. With each step, her anxiety got worse, and her lungs were aching from holding her breath. Her bottom lip was sore from where her teeth were constantly chewing on it.

The torch chased before them, barely touching the darkness and it was as if they were walking through a filtered landscape that was always a little darker than it should be.

Gail wanted to grab hold of Jesse's hand. It would give her comfort, give her courage and yet she knew she must not. If he suspected how scared she was, she thought that he would send her away. Possibly even drive her up to the pub. Even though that was exactly what she wanted she knew it was not what she needed, not what they needed. So, she gritted her teeth, bit down on her lip and followed him through the dreadful dark and dreary cellar.

"The EMF has stopped," Jesse's voice scared her and she jumped behind him.

"Sorry," he said with amusement in his voice. "I know it can get pretty scary down in the dark, but you have nothing to fear. In most houses the cellar is the hub of activity, in others, it can be the attic. These are the places we tend to hide our secrets. These are the places the bodies are buried. However, I'm not feeling anything here... maybe this is just another hoax after all."

"Are you sure?" Gail asked as she could not believe that he did not feel what she did. Maybe he was just saying that to make her feel better.

"We will have a look around, I will check all the floor and maybe later bring down some more equipment. But at the moment, this just feels like a cellar."

Gail wondered if she should say something. Would he think her silly? Was it just the tumor? She toyed with the idea as they walked further into the cellar. Something scuttled ahead of them and she ran back so quick she bumped into the wall.

"Don't worry, it was just a rat." Jesse was laughing a little as he said the words.

"Just a rat! Since when was a rat just a rat?" Gail also laughed, but it was more nerves than humor. The thought of the creepy rat riddled with fleas and disease made her shudder. If they were down here what about upstairs? How would she ever sleep knowing there were rats in the building?

The Haunting of Seafield House

"There's something here," Jesse said, and he moved forward so quickly that Gail was shrouded in darkness.

Her heart hammering she raced after him. Jesse was on his knees. He had pulled a small trowel from his pocket and was digging in the ground. Digging where the rat had been running. For a moment Gail felt sick, she wanted to just turn and run, and yet she knew she could not.

"What have you found?" she asked.

"I think we have bones," Jesse said, his voice high with excitement.

"Bones?" Surely he meant chicken bones or lamb bones... there was no way he could mean human bones.

Jesse let out a big sigh and stood up.

"It looks like it's just a dog."

"A dog!?" Gail could not get her head around what he meant.

"It looks like someone buried their dog down here," Jesse said as he brushed the soil off his hands. "Let's look a little further."

Looking further was the last thing that Gail wanted, and yet she followed him deeper into the cellar.

At the farthest corner, they found some old boxes. They looked like they had been there for years and were stacked three high and four deep. The bottom ones had obviously succumbed to damp and were leaning precariously with the weight on top of them.

Jesse rushed to them and began to open the first box.

"This could be something," he said as he pulled out clothes and a then an ancient looking journal. Turning the pages, he leaned over and was scanning down the pages. "This is from the 1800's... it is hard to read, but it looks like it shows the history of the original family."

"Maybe we should take it upstairs and read it in comfort?"

Jesse turned and blinded her for a moment, she screwed up her eyes and raised a hand to try and stop the pain. It did little good, and she felt a wave of nausea roll over her.

"This is really good, it looks like it was written by the woman who was killed here, Jenny Thornton."

Jesse was reading the journal, she could see his lips move as he struggled to make out the words and she wanted to shout at him to move. To take it back upstairs, away from the stench of decay and the feeling of pressure that was building all around her. As she watched Jesse read, she could feel the hairs on her arms stand up, the air cooled, and she shivered, and yet Jesse seemed to notice nothing. What was wrong with him?

"It talks about a child," Jesse said. "Oh, this is good, it looks like the child was... I think maybe it was hidden."

As Jesse spoke Gail felt the pressure increase, something whispered across her ear. It was just a touch, almost like a gust of air but she jumped back, and her hands flapped wildly at her head.

"What is it?" Jesse asked and grabbed her arm.

"I just feel something," she said.

Suddenly, his eyes were serious. "What do you feel?"

Gail took a breath and felt the hairs on her arms go down, and the pressure eased. How could she know if this was her illness or the house... or a ghost? Searching her mind, she tried to remember all the symptoms the doctor said she would have. Headaches were obvious, they had been the reason for her visit. He had also mentioned that she could go dizzy and that in a few weeks she would have to stop driving. Then there were going to be hallucinations, and what else? It was so hard to remember.

"Gail," Jesse spoke softly but the word was like a lifeline, and it brought her back to the present.

"I'm sorry," she managed. "It's like a pressure. Like I can feel that someone is here but can't quite see them. Then, it is hard to breathe, or the air is cold, sometimes I can almost hear whispers, and I don't know whether it is all in my head." Suddenly, she was crying, and Jesse pulled her into his arms. Leaning against his chest, she sobbed and clutched onto his shirt. It felt so good as he put his arms around her and gently rubbed her back.

Gradually she started to relax, and the tears slowed down.

"There, there," he whispered into her ear. "It's all okay, don't you worry now, nothing can hurt you."

The words broke her heart, and she cried again, almost wailing into his shirt as the warm salty tears streamed down her face. What was she to do? Maybe now was the time to tell him?

To explain why she was so on edge. Swallowing, she knew she was right. This was the moment. Maybe it would spoil the weekend, the house he had worked so hard to find, but suddenly it didn't matter. There was nothing more important to her than telling him how she felt. So she pushed back and smiled up at his face. It was mainly in shadow as the head torch was shining off to the right. It created a ghostly visage, and suddenly she wanted to laugh. Before she could, an almighty crash heralded from above. It sounded as if something was throwing things against the wall.

CRASH, CRASH, CRASH.

Over and over the noise rang through the house and Gail swore that she could feel the concussion of whatever was making that awful noise. Jesse had pulled her into him and was holding her close again. She could feel a slight shake of his hands before he clamped them to her and spun her around behind him.

Gail felt the breath catch in her throat, and her knees were weak. Jesse started to pull away. She grabbed his shirt and pulled him back. "What was it?"

Jesse was already heading across the cellar. All she could see was a moving patch of light, and she was suddenly engulfed in the dark. What should she do? Stay here in the dark and the whispers or follow him to whatever made the noise?

As Jesse reached the stairs and the light faded even more, she knew she could not stay and began to run for the last remaining spot of light. Would she make it before he was up the stairs and she was left in total darkness?

Chapter Six

"Jesse, just wait," Gail shouted as she raced across the dark cellar. Her feet stumbled and caught in the dirt, and she was pitched forward. Thrusting her arms out before her she fell against the wall. The dim light was to her left bouncing as Jesse took the stairs two at a time. She could hear the sound of his footsteps as they slap, slap, slapped on the concrete steps. Turning, she followed the light. It was hard to climb in the darkness. The steps were uneven, and she slipped and skinned her knee on the concrete. Once more cobwebs traced across her face and she had to fight hard to not scream and tear at them.

"Jesse, please wait," she shouted at Jesse but he was already turning the corner, and the stairway was plunged into blackness.

Gail felt as if a hand squeezed her heart and she could hear whispers all around her. It was impossible to tell what they were saying, but it felt like a threat. The sibilant hiss drove her on, and she picked herself up and crouched over. Using her hands to help, she made her way up the stairs like an animal. At the top, she turned left, and she could see the light in the hallway from the kitchen. It was enough to show her the route, to show her there were no obstacles. Now she was out of that awful hole, she felt as if the pressure had been released and the house was once more silent, she ran across the kitchen and into the hallway.

The lamp had been thrown to the floor and cast strange shadows. Equipment had been tossed around the room. There were tripods on the floor video cameras, and still cameras were discarded against the wall. Recording devices were strewn across the ground, and Jesse stood in the middle just staring.

Gail's heart was pounding, her hands were sweating, and she was gasping for breath, and yet Jesse looked completely calm. Was this something he was used to?

"What happened?" she asked.

Jesse turned to face her, his expression was strangely blank, and then it changed, and he put a smile on his face.

The Haunting of Seafield House

"I think it was just the wind," he said and pointed to the door.

That was when Gail noticed that the door was open and yet she could not feel a breeze through it. How much wind would have been needed to throw the heavy cameras off their purpose-built tripods? It didn't make sense, and she had had enough. The house didn't want them here, it was time to leave.

"I think we should go," she said.

"I can't leave now," Jesse said as he started picking up the equipment.

"Something wants to hurt us, something wants us gone," Gail knew she sounded desperate. She grabbed his arm and tried to pull him towards the door.

Jesse shook his arm free and took her hand in his. "This can't have been a spirit or any form of entity," he said. "The EMF meter worked in the kitchen but it showed nothing here, and it showed nothing in the cellar. That means there is something in the kitchen that is affecting the gauge. It is more than likely a power line outside, or a power line running under the house." The disappointment was plain on his face. "However, there are things I want to investigate here, this journal that I need to read." He showed her the book he had found in the cellar. "Maybe I can still find something, but it is nothing that means we have to leave, it is nothing to be scared of."

Gail looked at the smashed cameras and the debris that had been thrown around the room. "How can you say that?" she asked. "Is this really worth putting our lives at risk?"

Jesse looked at her with such a pained expression that she flinched away from him.

"How can you say that?" he asked. "You know how important this is to me, you know how long I've worked on this, and now, when I suddenly find the real thing you want to destroy it for me."

"That's just not true," she said. "I would do anything for you, and you know that."

"Then stop being such a whiny bitch and help me investigate this house." Jesse turned away from her and started picking up the equipment.

Gail did not know what to do, this was not like him, not like him at all. Jesse never swore and never even raised his voice at her. Was it the house making him this way? Was he feeling the same pressure as she was, or was she really just letting him down?

As she watched, Jesse picked up the equipment and reset it around the house. Then he walked over to the door and slammed it shut. Pulling the key from his pocket, he locked the door, dropped the key back in his pocket and walked into the room where they were to spend the night, all without saying another word.

Gail didn't know what to do. Though she wanted to leave, something told her it was the wrong thing to do. Somehow, she knew that she shouldn't leave Jesse alone and that she would be needed to help him. Apart from which they needed this time together, they needed this memory for what was to come. How would he cope when she told him? A shiver ran through her, only it was just the cold air, nothing felt wrong, and maybe she had just let her imagination run away with her. Maybe!

A beep from her watch told her it was time she could take some more painkillers, so she walked into the room and found her rucksack. In it were a bottle of water and the tablets. Quickly, she swallowed two of them and then went and sat next to Jesse.

"I'm sorry," she said. "This is all new to me, and it's a little bit scary... But I will do whatever you need. So what do we do next?"

Jesse looked up and smiled. "Why don't you make a drink while I read a little of this and then we will look upstairs."

Gail nodded, somehow she had expected an apology. Jesse never swore at her, never raised his voice and for a moment she felt angry. He should be more understanding, and then she realized. The last few weeks she had been secretive. How many times had she lied to him? It was a lot more than she liked and now she was keeping the biggest lie of all. Maybe he thought she was cheating, maybe he knew something was wrong and was just waiting for her to tell him.

Suddenly, that was exactly what she wanted to do, and yet she knew it was not the right time. So, she smiled and, getting out the camping stove, she started to make them some coffee.

In the corner, she could see the laptop, it rotated through views from all the cameras downstairs. It was just an empty house, there was nothing there.

Chapter Seven

Jesse read the book as Gail prepared the drinks. The more he read, the more excited he got. It was as if he was coming alive again, coming back to the man she knew and leaving behind the surly guy who had so recently shouted at her. The color came back to his cheeks, and his eyes were focused, his expression determined. Suddenly, all her fears seemed so silly. Gail had never believed in ghosts even though she knew Jesse did. It all seemed so foolish to her, but she had kept her peace throughout their years together. Now, her first time in a cold and drafty basement, her first time left alone in the dark and she had panicked. For a moment she thought about laughing. Only, she knew that would annoy him. So, she sipped her coffee, pulled on a thicker fleece and warmed her hands on her coffee.

Jesse was still reading, mouthing out the words which also made her want to laugh. She stifled the urge and shuffled on the floor, trying to get comfortable. It wasn't easy. Jesse seemed oblivious to her presence and totally at ease, his back against the wall, his legs out in front of him.

It was lighter in this room. They had three lamps, and just the brightness made her feel a little better. Yet it was so quiet. Gail liked to talk or to have on music, the silence was deafening.

"Don't forget your coffee," she said. "It will go cold."

Jesse grunted but did not take his eyes from the book.

"Does it help at all?" Gail asked.

Jesse looked up, and there was a hint of anger in his eyes. It caused her to gasp and then it was gone. It was as if her audible release of air had reminded him who she was.

"It's the diary, journal if you will, of Jenny Thornton. It's strange and confusing, but I think she had a daughter and either the child was killed by her husband or kept a prisoner. Maybe even both."

"That's awful," Gail said, and she could not help but shiver.

"The other possibility is that Jenny was deranged... but either way, it leads me to believe that the haunting will be upstairs. From what I can gather, it should be strongest in the front left bedroom."

Gail clung onto her coffee as a shudder ran through her. That was the room she had seen the girl in, and yet she was sure that was just a shadow.

Jesse put down the book and picked up his coffee. He drank it in one go and put the cup back down. "Are you ready?"

Gail nodded and took a last sip of her own drink before reluctantly letting go of the hot liquid and getting to her feet. To be honest, the last thing she wanted to do was leave that room, but she was here, and she would see this through.

"Do you know the girl's name?" she asked.

Jesse shook his head. "Not yet, though I'm sure it will be in here. To be honest, it is written in old English and is very faded, so it is hard to decipher."

Gail suddenly laughed. "So that's why you were mouthing the words, and here I was thinking they were just longer than one syllable."

Jesse laughed as he picked up his head torch and camera. It was a reference to him reading for his friend's child. The little boy, Jake, was always amused if he moved his lips and so Jesse made sure that he exaggerated it quite comically, only Mark, his friend, had always made fun of him.

Fixing the torch/camera unit onto his head, Jesse gave her a hurt expression which changed into a big grin. "Are you ready?" he asked.

Gail wanted to say no, she wanted to stay in the light room, instead, she nodded and said, "I ain't afraid of no ghosts."

"Really!" Jesse laughed and took her hand before leading her out of the room. That simple contact made her feel so much better. Suddenly, all her worries and fears were gone. Even if there was a spirit in this house, she was safe. After all, Jesse was the expert.

They crossed the hallway, where the equipment all stood silent. Lights flashed, the blue beam dissected the dark, but there was nothing to see. They turned towards the stairs, and it seemed so much darker there.

Letting go of her hand, Jesse went first. The stairs were bare, and the paint on the walls was peeling and flaking off. As he made his way to the first step, he shone the headlamp up the stairs, and to Gail, it looked as if the shadows drew back to escape the light. She really was letting her imagination run wild.

"Are they safe?" Gail asked as she looked at the old wood. It had crumbled in places, and she feared that it would not hold them.

"I will go first and test each step. To be honest, they don't look bad, and I have climbed much worse. Just stay close and be careful."

Without any hesitation, he started to climb the stairs. They creaked beneath his weight but held, and he did not stop and wait. Gail put her foot on one step and tested it with her weight. It creaked and gave a little but held firm. By this time Jesse was already half way up the stairs, and she had no choice but to follow more quickly. Each step gave a little, and she inched her way from one to the other expecting that they would snap at any moment. Only, they held her weight and soon she was on the landing and following Jesse as his torch splayed light across the walls.

At the top of the stairs, Jesse turned to the left, and Gail felt her heart sink. The thought of going to that left-hand room filled her with dread, even though she tried to tell herself she had not seen a girl, it was just a trick of the light. As they walked along the corridor Jesse was waving the EMF meter back-and-forth, just like he had been all the time, and yet she could tell that he was stressed. The wooden floor was carpeted, and it felt spongy beneath her feet. Not in a good way, not in a way that denoted expensive carpet and thick underlay... there was something slick and wrong about the feeling. It was as if she was walking on something rotten. Once again it seemed her imagination was getting the better of her. Of course, the carpet was old and had probably got damp and was maybe growing some form of moss or lichen, that was all it would be.

"Is something wrong? she asked.

Jesse just sighed and kept on walking. "I expected some readings up here, and yet there is nothing," he said after a few steps.

Behind her, the darkness seemed to wait with eager anticipation, in front was the shadow of his back. The small light of the head torch could barely cut through the darkness, Gail hurried to keep up. There were two doors up ahead of them, both on the left-hand side. Jesse tried the handle of the first, the door was locked. He sighed in frustration and moved on down the corridor. There was a window at the far end of the hallway, and yet no light shone through. Occasionally, the torch would hit it at just the right angle and would show their bleak

The Haunting of Seafield House

and wavery reflection. Gail knew there were no streetlights, the house was too remote and yet she imagined there would be some ambient light from the moon, but there was none. They came to the second door, and this time Jesse turned around and traced the meter around the frame. Another sigh and he carried on down the corridor.

As he got to the end again, he swept the meter around the window and the walls, but there was nothing. It made no sound, and as he turned, she could see that the needle was sat at the bottom of the gauge. Surely that was a good thing. She did not want there to be a spirit here, and yet the hair on the back of her neck was standing on end, and the place felt wrong. She could not shake the feeling that she was being watched, judged, but that had to be silly. After all, if there was anything here, Jesse would know about it.

"I really expected... something," Jesse said. He was staring at the gauge. As she watched he twiddled the dials, turned it off and then back on again and then shook it, but still, nothing happened. Slowly, not looking where he was going he retraced their route.

"Maybe if we tried the bedrooms," Gail said, and yet that was the last thing she wanted to do.

Jesse nodded and reached for the handle. Gail held her breath and bit her lip as she waited. Time seemed to slow down, and once more she felt the hair on the back of her neck rise, goosebumps traced down her arms, and she pulled the fleece tighter around her shoulders. It must just be cold.

The handle turned, and yet the door would not open. Jesse walked on to the next door, and Gail let out a sigh of relief. Somehow she knew that they had passed the worst of the danger.

Jesse tried the handle on the first door, and it was the same. The handle turned, but nothing happened. He dug into his pocket and pulled out the key for the front door. Tilting his head, he gave her an *it's worth a try* look and pushed the key into the lock. To both their surprise it went in, and they heard the mechanism move as he turned the key.

Giving her a smile he tried to open the door but nothing happened. It was wedged tight. Jesse rattled the handle and pushed harder and then grunted with the effort.

All Gail could think was *thank you*. For some reason, she did not want to go into that room. Jesse gave her another look, with a grin and then he leaned his shoulder on the door and pushed hard. For a moment, nothing happened, and then the door swung open, and he was sent tumbling inward. A blast of ice cold air shot from the room and Gail was shoved backward until she hit the wall. The shock knocked the air from her lungs, and she slumped to the floor gasping for breath.

Jesse had not noticed. As she lay on the floor, she could hear him walking away across a wooden floor.

Afraid for him, Gail took a deep breath and struggled to her feet. She was expecting the move to cause a wave of pain through her head and was relieved and surprised when it didn't happen.

Quickly, she followed him into the room. Something had pushed her. Maybe now he would understand, and they could leave. Eager to tell him what happened she went through the door to see Jesse walking along the far wall. There was a red dot from a camera just near the door. He had fixed the little camera to the wall, and it would be recording what happened on the laptop below.

Jesse looked very disappointed. Once more, the EMF detector was eerily silent.

"I can't understand it, there's nothing here," Jesse said without even looking up.

"Are you sure?" Gail asked. How could she explain what had just happened, when it hardly made sense, even to her. "Did you feel the force when you opened the door?" she asked weakly.

Jesse looked up, his eyebrows drawn together in question.

"I felt nothing. The door had swollen and jammed shut... when it opened, I fell through. I imagine you just felt the displacement of air."

"Jesse, I was slammed against the wall so hard that it knocked the breath from me."

Jesse came to her and put an arm on her shoulder. "Are you sure?"

Gail could not help but laugh. "It's not the sort of thing you get mixed up about. I feel something, I feel a presence here..." What she wanted to say was that she wanted to leave. That she felt unsafe, felt something dangerous and yet the look in his eye was not fear but excitement, and so she kept quiet. After all, it could just be her tumor, it was possible she was simply seeing things.

"Are you sure you're okay?" he asked.

Gail nodded. "I'll survive." As soon as she had said the word, she felt tears pricking at the back of her eyes. For the problem was she wouldn't survive. The tumor that was eating away at her head was terminal. The doctor had said she had no more than six months. Blinking back the tears she walked over to the window, to put some space between them. As she looked out the window, she felt a chill. It was not just cold but a dark presence, almost a weight pushing her toward that silvered pane. As a breath caught in her throat, she turned to say something but the words were cut off by the sound of a child crying. It was eerily clear in the stillness of the night, and she looked at Jesse to see if he heard it too.

"Did you hear that?" Jesse asked.

Gail nodded, at least that was not a figment of her imagination. Before she could say any more, Jesse was walking across the room leaving her in darkness. The shadows seemed to wrap around her like a cold cloak. It chilled her to the bone and made her feel lethargic and weak. And yet her heart was pounding so fast that she felt like she had just run a hundred yard sprint, only now, her legs refused to move. They felt weak, stiff, and as if her knees would buckle at any moment.

Jesse was on the stairs now, and the room was totally dark. Her feeling of dread intensified and suddenly she was able to move. Quickly, she crossed the room and stepped onto the stairs. Jesse was almost at the bottom, there was little light and what there was, was bouncing so much that she felt dizzy as she put her feet on the steps. She reached out for a handrail, but she couldn't find one. Instead, her fingers touched the wall. She expected flaking paint, and yet it felt slick, almost wet, and pulling her hand back a feeling of revulsion passed over her. Despite the danger of the stairs and the fact that she could not see, she rushed downwards towards the sound of the crying child.

It was a pitiful sound. One of pain and loss and sorrow and it made her stomach churn that someone could be in such pain. At last, she was down the stairs. Her mouth fell open to see a young girl, sitting in the middle of all the equipment.

Chapter Eight

Who was she? What was she and how had she got here?

Strangely, Gail felt afraid of the young girl. She looked about eight, with long brown hair that reached well past her shoulders and a long pale face. Dark eyes were wide and startled, and yet to Gail, there was a knowing in them. The child's clothes were also strange. She wore a rough brown dress that came down to her ankles, and it was covered with a white and yet stained pinafore. Who dressed like this? All she could do was stare, as a feeling of deep unease came over her.

"Hey, little girl," Jesse said as he walked towards her.

The girl backed away a few steps out of the circle of light and into the shadows at the edge of the room. For some reason, Gail felt better because she could no longer see her as well.

"You don't have to worry," Jesse said, his voice was calm, slow and low. It was comforting and encouraging. "My name is Jesse, what's yours?"

The girl shook her head but did not talk. Jesse dropped down to his knees and pulled a bar of chocolate from out of his pocket.

"Are you hungry?" he asked.

She nodded.

"This is really good." Jesse peeled the wrapper back off the bar and offered it to her.

Quick as lightning, her hand flew out and snatched the bar from him. Just as she did so the EMF meter that was on the floor and several of the other machines started to buzz. Gail could see the needle on the meter as it hit the red line and then bounced again and again and again. Other equipment was also vibrating and flashing to warn them of something, Gail wished she knew of what.

The child took a bite of the chocolate bar but did not seem to chew it and just stood there

The Haunting of Seafield House

staring at them while the equipment went crazy.

Jesse picked up the EMF and then walked across to some of the machinery. He flicked buttons, turned dials and checked on displays. The smile on his face was real and spoke of pure excitement. What did it mean?

As quickly as it started all of the equipment stopped, and Jesse seemed to crumple in front of them.

Gail was still afraid of the child. Who was she? What was she? What was she doing here? All of these questions were buzzing around her mind, and she could not find a decent answer to any of them.

Now the house was silent again, Jesse turned back to the girl. "It is very late, what are you doing here?"

"I'm looking for my parents," she said.

"Why would your parents be here?" Jesse asked.

"It was all a mistake," she said.

"Hey, honey, what was a mistake?" Jesse said as he inched slowly towards her.

The closer he got the more uncomfortable Gail felt, she wanted this girl out of here and she wanted her... no, it, gone now.

"Tell us where you live," she said and drew a sharp look from Jesse. Maybe it had come out a little harsh, but somehow she knew their life depended on getting this girl out of the house.

Gail did just what Jesse had and lowered herself to the floor sitting in front of the child.

"I'm Gail, and this is Jesse. We don't want to hurt you but it's late and dark, and we need to get you home. Tell us your name, and we will take you home to your parents."

The girl started to cry again and let out a wail that seemed to rattle Gail's teeth and turn her stomach.

Jesse turned to her again and this time gave her one of his *now look what you've done* looks. At that moment, she wanted to slap him, to just grab him by the shoulders and pull him into the car and then to drive away to safety. Yet she knew that if she said anything that he would just laugh at her and then maybe think she was trying to destroy his dreams.

So she did something she really did not want to do. Reaching out a shaking hand she touched the girl's shoulder. At that moment of contact she expected her fingers to sink right through, only they didn't. The child was flesh and blood, and she was freezing.

"Jesse, grab a sleeping bag," she said. "We need to get you warm and then to take you home. Come on, tell us where you live."

The child's tears stopped almost as quickly as they had started and she looked up with big liquid eyes. Her bottom lip was quivering, and she was trying hard to gain control... and yet Gail could swear that she could see triumph in her eyes. Hiding just beyond the surface was something that scared her more than she could say.

"They're not there," the girl snapped in a weak and yet forceful voice. "They left me all alone, and I don't want to be alone anymore."

Gail could sense Jesse's anger, and she felt annoyed herself. How could parents do this to a child? How could they leave it alone and afraid? It didn't bear thinking of. Why could she not think of the child as a girl, a her? Why was she always an it?

"Well, you can stay here with us the night," Jesse said.

In her mind, Gail screamed no, but the words never came out.

For some reason, Jesse explained to the child what they were doing and why they were there. Then he suggested that Gail stay with her and comfort her while he continued to search the house. Just the thought of being alone with the child sent cold shivers down Gail's back, and she knew she could not do it.

"Why don't we stick together?" Gail asked.

The child nodded her head in agreement.

Gail could see Jesse thinking. She knew he wondered if they should leave or if they should just stay together and yet the pull of the house was calling him. This was his dream, this was what he had worked for, and he was not going to give up on this opportunity. So, in the end, he nodded, and he found a jacket for the girl, wrapping her in it until she was warm and comfortable.

"I want to check out the other bedrooms," Jesse said. "This time I want you to have a lantern, Gail. And we will stick close together."

At least that was something that Gail could agree with, so, she collected one of the lanterns and was ready to follow Jesse. Something ice cold touched her fingers, and she looked down to see the child grasping onto her hand. Every fiber of her being wanted to pull away, wanted to shake the cold icy appendage from her fingers, and yet she knew she could not. So, she smiled a weak smile and then turned to follow Jesse.

It was easier going up the stairs with a lantern and a lot less scary but the child would not let go of her fingers. The cold from that touch seemed to spread up her left arm and had seeped into the bone of her shoulder. It was so bad that her clavicle ached and throbbed as if frozen.

"What's your name, honey?" Gail asked. It wasn't really because she wanted to know but because she found it strange not knowing and she wanted to hear her own voice.

"Sarah," the young girl said in a voice that was barely a whisper.

"Sarah, that's a nice name. What's your second name?" At last, she was getting somewhere, and Gail couldn't seem to stop asking.

"Thornton," Sarah said.

Gail didn't know why but that name sent a shiver down her spine. Where had she heard it before? What did it mean?

They had all reached the top of the stairs, and they turned left. Jesse walked past the first door and went to the second. The dreaded room. This time the handle turned, and the door opened away from them. He gave a smile before stepping inside. Fading paper hung from the walls. It was some form of relief pattern and was pale yellow washed out to almost white. The bedroom was furnished, with a small bed, a wardrobe and a chest of drawers. Jesse walked to the bed holding the meter out before him, but there was nothing, nothing at all.

Gail stood in the middle of the room with Sarah clutching her hand. By now her whole arm was enveloped in a deep ache, and she found it hard to move. It was as if the appendage had simply frozen. She watched as Jesse walked to the bed and then past it. As always, he was testing with the EMF meter, but nothing was registering, and yet she could hear whispers. Turning around she looked for where they had come from... but there was nothing, and now they seemed to be all around her.

"Jesse, do you hear that?" she asked.

"Can't hear anything, what is it?"

"It's like the whispering of a crowd... as if they are just too far away for me to hear them."

As she glanced around the room searching for the whispers, she noticed footprints in the dust of the floor and her heart nearly stopped. They were small barefooted prints that were obviously that of a child. The footsteps led from the hallway directly up to Sarah. Had Sarah been here all this time? Were they her footprints they had seen earlier? It didn't make sense but who else could have left them?

"Sarah, how long have you been at this house?" Gail asked. Out of the corner of her eyes, she could see Jesse walking around the room. He had reached the chest of drawers and pulled one open.

"Always?" Sarah said.

What did she mean? Gail turned to speak to Jesse, and the temperature seemed to drop in the room. She yanked her hand free from Sarah's and hugged her arms. It felt like static running across her, raising the hairs on her neck, her arms, and even her scalp. Jesse seemed to have noticed nothing, and the EMF device in his hand was silent.

Gail did not know what to do. Surely Sarah was lying or telling tales, surely she had not been here all night? Or had she? The pressure in the room seemed to increase and Gail was finding it harder to breathe. She watched Jesse open the wardrobe door. Leaning around it, he looked inside and pulled back and turned away.

Dirt smeared hands reached out of the dark wardrobe. There was at least a dozen of them grasping, clutching, and grabbing for Jesse. They seemed to writhe and undulate, their fingers opening and closing hungrily as they got closer and closer to him.

Gail let out a shriek.

As he heard her, Jesse turned quickly and pulled away just in time to avoid the hands. They shrank back into the cupboard, and she wondered if they had been real. If she had seen them or if they were just in her mind.

BANG.

The bedroom door slammed closed and then flew open crashing into the wall behind it.

BANG.

It slammed closed again and then flew open.

BANG, BANG.

"Jesse!" Gail pleaded for an explanation.

Jesse was looking at the door with an expression of rapture. He glanced down at the EMF and then shook it. There was nothing, it was as if it was dead.

"I don't think this is working," he said as he approached Gail and started walking towards the door.

The door kept slamming, open and closed, open and closed.

"We have to get out of here," Gail said as her eyes swept from the door to the wardrobe and back again. The hands had gone, and yet the inside of the cupboard was much darker than it should have been. It was like a void, like a pit, like an entrance into somewhere evil.

"We don't need to leave," Jesse said. "We need to document this, to record it, to investigate what is causing it. You have to realize this will make my career. With this behind me, I can do anything."

Gail swallowed, she wanted to say *only if we get out alive* but the words would not come. Yet she knew she had to do something, maybe if she took the child away, maybe the house would be calmer. It was a strange thought to have, and yet somehow she believed it. So she opened her mouth and was about to tell Jesse just that when a voice in the room silenced her.

"... the girl," the voice hissed like static on the radio.

Gail noticed Jesse was looking around.

"Did you hear that?"

Jesse nodded.

"What about the girl?" he asked.

The hissing rose and faded like a wave on the air. There were voices in it, words in it that they could just make out...

"Sarah." Was one and there was, "pain... torment." But they could not make out complete sentences. The rest was just static on the air, and she could see that Jesse was getting frustrated.

Again he turned the EMF off and as he turned it back on it sparked violently and flew from his hand.

"Jesse!" Gail screamed.

Jesse staggered, his arm held out before him, his hand looked to have been seared with smoke. For a moment, he seemed to overbalance to stumble backward, and as he righted himself, he overbalanced and dropped onto his stomach. As he hit the floor, the door stopped slamming, and the pressure eased. Whatever had been there Gail knew it was gone.

Fear coursed through her and she screamed out his name, "Jesse!"

Chapter Nine

Gail felt her world dissolve as she watched Jesse fall. What had happened to him? What would she do if she lost him? She dropped to her knees at his side and grabbed hold of his arm, automatically searching for a pulse. Jesse's eyes were closed, but as she touched him, they opened. The pupils dilated wide and looked black against the gray, slowly they focused, and he smiled up at her. Relief was like spring sunshine after a winter storm, and she pulled him into her arms.

"Jesse, Jesse, oh, my God, are you all right?"

Jesse nodded and began to sit up.

"I'm fine." He looked down at his right hand, there was a small burn, and it was blackened with smoke, and yet the smile on his face got big enough to light up the room.

"Did you see that?" he asked. "That was just amazing."

Gail nodded. "I saw it, and I heard it... and I saw hands in the cupboard reaching out to grab you... we need to leave, we need to get out of here as quick as we can. Can you stand yet?"

Jesse started to get to his feet, and Gail offered him her arm. He seemed fine and was steady once he was on his feet.

"We can't leave, not now," he said with a look of astonishment on his face. "This is exactly what I've been searching for. I need to get the better camera and document as much of this as I can."

Gail was overwhelmed with fear. Maybe it was the tumor, maybe it was her impending death, but she did not want this, and she did not think she could continue to search this house.

"I can't," Gail said. The fear in her voice shamed her, but she could not hide it. "I'm frightened and I don't want to do this anymore."

The Haunting of Seafield House

Jesse turned to look at her and reached out a hand to her cheek. He caressed her gently and pulled her close, so they were leaning forehead to forehead.

"I understand," he said as his fingers circled the back of her neck. The gentle touch relaxed her as it always did. She could smell him, and it felt so comfortable, so normal and so safe.

"I won't make you stay," he said, "but I would prefer it if you did. Why don't I take you and Sarah back down to the room where our things are. I brought a bottle of wine... in case we needed to celebrate. Why don't you have a glass and stay in that room... just you two together, while I look around a bit more?"

Gail wanted to say no, she wanted to leave, to go home, to go to the pub, she didn't mind which. Yet a glance at her watch told her it was three in the morning, there was not much of the night left. Maybe she could stay until morning, maybe that would be all right. She glanced at Sarah, not sure if she wanted to be in the same room as the pasty looking child. Something had changed, the girl looked better, healthier. Now, why would that be?

"I'll stay, but no more exploring and the next thing that goes wrong, we're leaving."

Jesse reached up and kissed her forehead and then pulled her into a hug. Gail relaxed into it for a moment and hugged him back and then she pulled herself from his arms and looked down at his hand.

"First, you need to let me look at this burn, we have a first-aid kit downstairs."

***

Gail tended to Jesse's hand. The burn was not too bad, so she applied some cream and a loose bandage, but she did not want to let it go. The fear of him leaving the room and searching the house... of him finding something, was so strong it was making it hard for her to breathe. Yet Jesse was simply excited, and she could see he was desperate to get back to exploring. Sitting still was never one of his strong points, and it amused her as he tried to rein in his enthusiasm, he was almost vibrating on the spot.

"I want you to check in with me every half an hour," she said as she let go of his hand.

Jesse was grinning like a party clown, as he grabbed the handheld camcorder. "I'll do my best," he said with a big grin and a wink. "But don't worry if I'm a little bit late, you know what it's like if things get exciting, I might not be able to come straight back down."

"What about the radios, or phones?" Gail asked.

"They may not work. If there is a lot of spiritual activity, it will interfere with the signals. Don't worry, I'll take one and if I can, I will message you. Look, Gail, just stop panicking, I'm a big boy, and I can look after myself."

The words crushed her a little bit, she did not panic, and yet she nodded. "I love you," she said and squeezed his arm.

"Ditto," he said with a laugh, a reference to his favorite film. Then he kissed her on the forehead.

Gail felt a deep sense of dread as Jesse left the room closing the door behind him. She had three lamps spread around the room, and it was well lit up. Yet still, she was afraid. In the corner, Sarah was sat on one of the sleeping bags. She was the quietest child Gail had ever known. Something suddenly struck her.

"Sarah, where's your phone?"

"We don't have a phone," Sarah said.

What child doesn't have a phone? For some reason, it made Gail even more uneasy and then she realized the girl didn't say I don't have a phone she said we don't have a phone. That didn't make sense at all.

***

The moment Jesse had left the room he felt his confidence leaving him. Though his equipment was not working, he didn't need it to tell him that there was something wrong in this house. Nevertheless, he put on a brave face in front of Gail because this was his dream, yet right at this moment he felt unsure. Maybe Gail was right, maybe they should just leave. Only that was childish, how many years had he worked for this moment, for a real haunted house and now Gail was trying to spoil it for him. She was trying to take it away from him, to stop him from discovering the most amazing discovery of all time.

Jesse walked towards the stairs, this time he didn't have a light, all he had was the camcorder, and with its infrared screen, the world was strangely monotone. The stairs creaked as he stepped onto them and he fought down a feeling of dread. Something was happening here, and it was his job to research it and record it, why was he not excited?

Slowly, he made his way up the stairs, using the strange green shaded screen to light

The Haunting of Seafield House

his way. The higher he went, the faster his heart pounded, and his breath was coming in short, sharp gasps. It was time to get a grip, to control himself. How many times had he told other people that spirits could not hurt them and yet here he was behaving like a virgin on his first ghost hunt?

It seemed to take an age to climb the stairs but eventually, he was at the top, only this time he turned right. There should be two more rooms on this side of the hallway. As he stepped forward, he passed through a cold spot and was instantly chilled to the bone. Something was here!

Panning the camcorder from side to side he held his breath and peered into the darkness. Something flashed across in front of him. It was nothing he could see, just an increase in the darkness. It simply became denser and harder to see and as quick as it had come the object was gone. Jesse turned left and right panning the camera across the hallway. Then a sense of dread overcame him, and he turned around. There was nothing behind him, and he let out a gasp of air, but as he did the camcorder died, and the house was plunged into darkness. Jesse turned back around expecting to be attacked from behind, he was backing away slowly towards the stairs, and he could hear something in front of him. It was the scraping of feet across the carpet, and it was coming towards him. The urge to flee, to escape the house was strong and yet he knew it was the wrong move to make. Fighting down his panic, he shook the camera and was amazed when the light came back on. In front of him, a young man and woman were cowering in the corner. The man had his arms around the woman and was holding her close. One hand was held up as if to ward off danger and his eyes were wide and terrified.

Jesse felt fear seep down his spine and into his knees and they seemed to buckle beneath him. Reaching out with a hand he grabbed onto the wall and steadied himself, he looked through the camcorder and was pleased to see it was recording. The couple both lifted their heads and turned to him, they seemed to be pleading, and then they looked over his head. They were looking behind him, and their eyes opened even wider and their mouths contorted into a silent scream.

Jesse wanted to turn around, he knew something was behind him, and he knew it was coming for him, but he could not take his eyes off the couple. The fear and pain on their faces was something he would remember for the rest of his life. Part of him wanted... felt compelled to help them, so he reached out a hand and then they were gone. They blinked out of existence as if they had never been there.

Jesse spun around but there was nothing behind him, the corridor was just an empty blank canvas painted on the camcorder's screen. He let out a breath and dropped to his knees on the spongy, damp carpet.

He had it, after all these years he had proof, and it filled him with both elation and fear.

He had proof!

Part of him wanted to go down and tell Gail, to explain that he had succeeded and that he was fine but another part of him was pulled onwards to find more.

So he got up and approached the first door, reaching out for the handle. He expected it to be locked, but it turned and opened easily, swinging silently inward. It was just an empty room with no furniture. The wallpaper was plain and had once been cream but was now stained in places. Tatty orange curtains were half hung at the window. It looked as if they had been yanked down at some point and they dangled forlornly across the window sill and onto the floor. The floor was simple wooden floorboards. There was nothing to see, and yet he felt compelled to investigate the room.

Coming into the room he walked all around it pointing the camcorder into every corner. When his back was to the door, it slammed shut behind him, and he jumped around expecting to see the couple there again or something worse. Only there was nothing... and he could feel a cold draft from the window behind him. Letting out a breath he laughed a little, it seemed like he was jumping at shadows.

Continuing his circle of the room he could hear whispers. Like a thousand voices just at the edge of his hearing. Though he strained as hard as he could none of the words were audible and he just hoped the camcorder was getting the sound. Even though he couldn't fully hear them, the voices raised his pulse and goosebumps rose on his arms. Suddenly, he wanted out of the room and did not want to hear what the voices wanted to tell him, so he strolled to the door and pushed a mobile camera into the wall. This time when he touched the handle, it burned his hand, and he pulled away quickly.

The voices were getting louder, and now he could pick out certain words, *betrayal*, *cheat*, *lying*.

Placing his hands over his ears, he tried to ignore them but the voices became more insistent, and soon they were inside his head. They were talking about Gail and about how she had changed, and suddenly he wanted to hear them.

"Where has she been?

"What has she been doing?"

"How many times has she lied to you?"

Jesse didn't want to hear it, Gail wouldn't lie to him, of that he was sure and yet the more the voices whispered, the more he began to believe them. She had been different recently, canceling lunch dates with him, leaving the room to make a phone call. How many times had she gone out recently and not really told him where she was going?

"She lied to you... She betrayed you," the voices whispered in his head.

"No," he said. "No, I don't believe it."

Yet the voices kept whispering, kept telling him and the more they did, the more he could see it. Gail had been lying to him, and it had been right under his nose. Then he remembered coming home just a week ago, and there was Gail with his best friend, Mark. They were sat together on the sofa. They had been holding hands and laughing, and when he walked into the room, Mark had jumped up as if he was nervous, as if he had been caught. Afterward, they had all laughed about it, and Mark had said he came to see him and yet even then it didn't sound true. Only, he never believed that Gail would cheat and so he thought nothing of it.

"They are cheating on you," the voices whispered. "You need to kill her."

Jesse felt anger inside him that he could not control. They were right, if she had done this then she needed to die. For just a moment his mind took control again, and everything seemed ridiculous, the thought of killing Gail was just so unbelievable that it sickened him, only then the voices started again, and he was under their control.

"Kill, kill, kill her, kiiiillll her, do it now."

Jesse looked down, and he had an eight-inch kitchen knife in his hand. The sight of it gave him great pleasure. He had a job to do.

Chapter Ten

Gail sat in the room drinking a glass of wine. Normally it would have relaxed her, but tonight she just felt more and more agitated. The LED lamps seemed to flicker from time to time which made no sense at all. They were battery lamps, a power fluctuation could not affect them, the breeze could not affect them and yet every now and then all of them flickered together. Each time it happened Gail felt as if her heart would simply stop, that it could not take any more of this and yet each time she got through it, even if her nerves were worn to the bone.

In the corner, Sarah had stared at her for some time, but at long last, she was now lying down and seemed to be asleep. Gail checked her watch, for the hundredth time, it had been over 35 minutes since Jesse left the room, where was he?

She had checked on the laptop, but all of the cameras were showing static. Jesse had told her not to worry about this. That if it happened, it was a good thing and that they would still be recording. However, it didn't make her feel better. If she could have seen him, then she would know he was safe. She picked up the radio and pressed the button, the red light glowed to tell her she could speak.

"Jesse, are you there?"

There was nothing but static, and when she pressed the button again, the light did not come on the radio. It was as if it was dead. Reaching into her pocket she pulled out her mobile, it too was dead and yet she knew the battery was fully charged.

Fear surrounded her, like a cold breeze it seemed to seep into her bones and weakened her. All she wanted to do was curl up in the sleeping bag or to grab the car keys and run from the house. Then she remembered Jesse had the key to the door. There was no way out of here unless he came back. That was a strange thought to have; of course, he was coming back, he was only looking around after all. She took another gulp of the wine and decided to wait 10 more minutes but then she would go find him.

The Haunting of Seafield House

Every minute seemed like an hour, and she started to pace the room. Her legs were weak, and she felt so tired that she had to sit down. Maybe it was a bad idea to go after him, she felt exhausted, lethargic, as if she would fall asleep at any moment. Suddenly, that frightened her, why would she be feeling tired when she was so terrified? Maybe it was the adrenaline, so many scares had drained her of adrenaline, and now she was coming down. It didn't matter, she couldn't wait any longer, she had to go find Jesse.

As she got up to leave she checked on Sarah, the child seemed to be sleeping. So, she picked up one of the lanterns and walked to the door. Slowly, carefully, trying to make as little noise as possible, she opened the door and went out into the corridor. The lantern cast shadows across the equipment and the large open hallway. Jesse had probably gone back upstairs, but she felt drawn to the kitchen and thought she would check there first. Feeling drained she made her way across the corridor, around the cameras and other equipment all of which were totally still and dark. The LEDs, the cameras and equipment no longer seemed to be working. It was as if the house was interfering with all electronic equipment. As if on cue her lamp flickered off, and she was plunged into darkness.

Gasping for breath, she turned on the spot expecting something to come out from behind her. There was nothing there that she could feel and the darkness was impenetrable. Panic rose in her chest like a clawing beast trying to escape. It was as if pressure was building inside of her.

"Oh, my God, oh, my God, oh, my God," she whispered and felt herself sink to her knees. As they touched the ground, the light came back on, and the room was empty. There was nothing there, nothing to be afraid of.

Slowly, she got to her feet and made her way toward the kitchen. Then she noticed there seemed to be more doors in the hallway. There had only been four before, she was sure of that, and yet now there were six. Surely, she must be mistaken, so she carried on and went into the kitchen. There were more doors here too, there were four now, and that just seemed wrong. Was she mistaken? Had she forgotten? Maybe it was the tumor for surely her architect's brain would not get something like that so wrong.

Her heart was racing now, her stomach was turning somersaults, and the skin on her arms tingled with goosebumps. There was something so wrong in this house, she had to find Jesse, and she had to get out of there quickly. Then she looked at the four doors in the kitchen, and she knew she must have made a mistake. There was no other explanation, nothing could make more doors, it just didn't make sense. It was obvious, she had just had the most devastating

The Haunting of Seafield House

news of her life, and her mind was playing tricks on her. Nothing could compare to what she had heard this morning, it was understandable that she was having a few problems. It must be the brain's way of coping with such horrendous and devastating news. Maybe it was the fear of having to tell Jesse, of having to let him down. Or the doors were a representation of the journey she was about to make. How many times was death depicted as an opening door?

Yet would that door open to light or darkness?

Shaking the thought away she knew it didn't matter, whatever it was, was not supernatural. Everything that happened tonight was all in her mind. She could almost believe it, could almost convince herself there was nothing wrong here. That is was just tall tales and a creepy old house. That her imagination was leading her down a path of its choosing.

"Jesse, Jesse," she called out, and the words echoed back to her in the empty house.

The sound was so desolate, so lonely that it filled her with despair and she had to swallow the lump in her throat.

The room smelled musty, a little rotten. The scent seemed to clog her throat and sent a shiver down her back. "Stop it," she admonished quietly. It was understandable. The house was old, vacant and obviously damp. Everything must have an explanation.

Then her eyes were drawn to one of the extra doors. It seemed to move, to shift to shimmer, as her breath caught in her throat the door swung open. Something brushed against her leg, and she jumped back with a scream. Her heart was beating so fast and yet she could not breathe, and for a moment she felt faint. Her arms flew out to her side to attempt to balance herself, and she heard the sound of a meow. It came from behind, and when she looked around, there was a cat sat there. It was a large tortoiseshell, sat on its haunches and licking its paws.

A nervous laugh burst from her.

"Cheers, Kitty, my heart really needed that workout." Gail laughed and turned back to the door. It opened onto blackness. The scent of decay grew, and the room seemed colder. She shrugged into her fleece and looked at the opening, it made her skin crawl, and her heart was beating faster, and yet it was just an empty room. A dark, empty room, and how she hated the dark. Suddenly, she wanted to find Jesse and to not be alone, he had to be upstairs, and so she turned.

The Haunting of Seafield House

The cat was still there, and as she watched, it walked into the wall and disappeared. Gail shook her head. She was hallucinating already... maybe she had less time than she thought.

Gail felt hands pushing against her chest. She was slammed backward so fast that her feet were lifted from the floor and she was rammed into the wall so hard it knocked the breath out of her. Something had her by the throat. It felt like a small hand that applied more pressure the more she struggled. Kicking out with her legs she tried to strike at her attacker, but there was nothing there. It was impossible to breathe and the more she kicked, the tighter the hand became. As her lungs screamed for air, she kicked hard, but she knew she was getting weaker. The lantern lay on its side on the floor and cast some faint light around the room and yet she could see nothing in front of her. Nothing was attacking her, and she felt herself start to fade. The pain in her throat as she dangled above the ground was all that was keeping her conscious. Her arms were forced back against the wall, and at first, she could not move them.

There was nothing she could do, and she felt as if she was sinking into a deep, warm ocean. Suddenly, she just wanted to give in. To let the warm blackness envelop her and to let go of this life. Maybe it was the best thing, maybe this was a better way to go. Just before she gave in, she saw Jesse's face, and she knew she could not leave him. Applying every last effort she had, she freed her arms and scrabbled about in front of her, but there was nothing to grab hold of. Her fingers scraped her throat, trying to free the pressure from it, to allow her to draw another sweet breath but there was nothing to grab onto. Tears were streaming down her eyes, they were hot against the skin, and still, she tried to move the fingers that were crushing her windpipe as panic threatened to overwhelm her.

Then she heard a voice in her head.

"Give in to the ffffear," it hissed like a snake, like static and chilled her to the bone.

"Beg for your worthlesssss life, or join us for eternity."

"Never!" she screamed and managed to drag in a tortured breath. It gave her more energy and boosted her spirit, and she fought harder kicking with her legs thrashing out with her arms.

"We will hhhhaaaave you," the voice said. "There is no eeessscape, not for you."

"What do you mean?" she shouted.

"We only neeeeeedddd one of you, the decision is yyyyyooooours."

The Haunting of Seafield House

With that, the pressure was released, and she dropped to the floor gasping for breath. All she really wanted to do was race from the room, but she could not stand. So she lay there, her hands feeling for the damage on her throat as she tried desperately to catch her breath. Tears were streaming down her face as she heard the words again. "We only need one of you, the decision is yours."

Wiping away tears she tried to stand. At first, she was dizzy, and her legs would not hold her. Yet she grabbed onto the wall and pulled herself to her feet. On shaky legs, she walked over and found the lantern. Under its comforting light, she could see blood under her fingernails. It must have come from her neck when she was trying to remove the hands, she must have scratched her own skin. It didn't matter, surely this would be enough to get Jesse to come to his senses. Turning to leave the kitchen she came face-to-face with Sarah. Just seeing her there set her heart pounding and she stepped back, afraid.

The child looked happy and was positively glowing when only a few hours ago she had looked like a sickly waif. For some reason seeing her looking so well disturbed Gail. Something was not right about this child. It didn't matter, for now, she had to find Jesse and tell him what had happened. They had to get out of there.

Sarah was stood in the doorway, and suddenly Gail wondered if she would let her leave.

Chapter Eleven

Gail knew she was being foolish, how could this child stop her from leaving? Though she looked stronger than when they had first met her, she was still a child, and yet there was a coldness in her eyes that filled Gail with panic. Trying to calm her breathing she walked towards Sarah. The girl stood in the center of the door a slight smile on her face. Only there was nothing pleasant about her. If anything, she looked threatening.

"Why don't we go find Jesse?" Gail said.

"I want to stay here." Sarah crossed her arms across her chest, and the smile on her face grew. Now it really looked threatening, and Gail wanted to shrink away from her. Yet she knew she couldn't, something told her Jesse's life depended on her staying strong.

Maybe if she found something out about the child, then maybe she could work out what was going on.

"Why don't you tell me about your parents," Gail asked, and instead of walking towards the door she backed away and leaned against the sink.

Sarah seemed to relax, and she came into the room a little bit, her eyes were still cold, dead and Gail could swear that they never blinked.

"I've had quite a few mummies and daddies... which one would you like to hear about?"

Gail could not help but gasp. It wasn't what she said it was the way she said it. It was so matter-of-fact, so empty of emotion. Maybe she was feeling the child's pain, or maybe she feared that Sarah had no pain. The panic was back. Somehow, she knew she didn't have long to save Jesse, and yet she felt she couldn't escape this room. Then she found herself hyperventilating. Desperate for every breath, and yet the harder and faster she breathed the more her lungs burned and the more lightheaded she felt. The doctor had warned her about this. He had told her that she could have panic attacks. For a moment, she almost laughed, as she was sure that this wasn't quite the circumstances that he meant.

The Haunting of Seafield House

The faster she breathed, the more anxiety she felt, the better Sarah seemed to look. It was almost as if the girl was feeding off of her fear. So, she forced herself to take a deep breath and gradually the panic started to fade. The sweet air in her lungs felt good, and her dizziness subsided a little. With control of her breath came control of her emotions and control of her mind. Having time to think put things in perspective and the more time she spent with Sarah, the more she believed that she was key to the house and their escape from it... or their capture in it for all time. Where did such a foolish thought come from?

"Tell me about your first parents?" she asked.

"Daddy used to hurt mummy," Sarah said, "and I didn't like it. There was an old woman living nearby. She brought me here, told me what to do. Only I was too scared then... but not now."

The coldness in her voice turned Gail's stomach, and she wanted her to stop, to just shut up but she knew that she had to hear more.

"Too scared of what?"

Sarah laughed, it wasn't the light, carefree laugh of a child but a dark, cold, animalistic noise that grated on Gail's nerves.

"Daddy pushed mummy from the window. It didn't kill her, though he thought it had. That was really funny. So I did the same to him."

Gail couldn't believe what she had heard, and she wanted to shout at her to stop.

"It was a long while before I had another mummy and daddy, but then I did. They were nice at first, but soon this new daddy became just like the old one. Always angry, always shouting, always looking for a knife. Do you want to hear what happened this time?"

Gail really didn't. She knew she should feel sorry for this child who had obviously suffered severe abuse and yet the more she heard, the more frightened of her she was.

"If you want to tell me, I'm happy to hear."

Sarah smiled, and yet her eyes stayed cold.

"It was 1969," Sarah said. "The night of the first moon landing and we were all excited."

"What?" Gail said so quietly that Sarah didn't hear.

"Only daddy got angry because mummy kept talking and then he started shouting. I remember watching, watching the shouting, watching the anger as he lost control. I remember him grabbing the knife and how he plunged it into mummy's chest time and time again. I counted 20 before I lost count and then the police came and I had to hide."

Gorge rose in Gail's throat, and she had to swallow hard to keep it down. "The police came, did they find you... and help you?" Even as she said the words, Gail wondered if it would have been the police that needed help.

"No, they found daddy," Sarah said and started laughing. "I knew they would never find me, but I knew that they would look. So I let them hear me crying and then when they came to look for me I invited daddy into my room. That's when I pushed him."

"No... Oh, my God, no," Gail said. "This has to be some form of a sick joke. The year is 2017 if you were alive in '69 then you would be 48 now. Stop this, stop lying, tell me what's really happening. Tell me where your parents are for I want to take you home."

Before Gail had even finished talking she could see the anger in Sarah's eyes. They turned almost black, and her face screwed up into a snarl.

"I got the timeline wrong," Sarah said, and the anger was clear in her voice. "I'm not supposed to tell you dates or times. I'm not supposed to let you be logical. Why don't you feel sorry for me?"

"Because you scare me," Gail said before she even realized it.

Sarah started to laugh, and laugh, and laugh and the sound of it set Gail's nerves on edge. She wanted to shout at her to shut up, to get out, to go back to wherever she came from and yet no words would come. Maybe she had made a mistake engaging the child... was she even a child? Suddenly, she worried about Jesse again, and she knew she had wasted too much time. She tried to walk around Sarah but as she did the child launched at her.

In the blink of an eye, Sarah had crossed the distance between them, and her small hands were around Gail's throat. Gail was carried back against the counter. It struck her in the kidneys with such force that she let out a gasp of air and her back was filled with a sharp pain that radiated down her legs.

The child's tiny hands were squeezing her windpipe. Gail tried to draw in a breath but she couldn't, and she remembered something else the doctor had said to her. Everyone needs help, whether you are religious or not, when things get bad ask for help. It had seemed such a strange thing to say at the time, but right now it felt like a lifeline. So she closed her eyes and asked for help. "Please, Lord, help me through this. Give me the strength to save Jesse for he is all that matters now." The pain in her throat

The Haunting of Seafield House

eased, and she dropped to the floor, she opened her eyes to find Sarah was gone.

Gail knew she had to run. That she must get out of the house as quickly as possible, only her feet would not move. Her head was pounding, the pain was so bad that it crushed her. All she wanted to do was curl up in the dark and stop the pain, and yet it was driving her onward. A wave of nausea and dizziness came over her, and she reached out to the wall to steady herself. It should have been hard and crusty with flaking paint, and yet it felt soft beneath her hands. As she leaned there gaining her breath and trying to control the pain, the wall moved beneath her fingers. It undulated and fluctuated, and she pulled her hand back as if it had been burnt. Staring at the wall, she could see faces appearing in the plaster. One would form and then disintegrate while another formed above it. Though she wanted to run she could not take her eyes off the strange phenomenon. Lifting the lantern, she played the light across the faces and could see the mouths opening and closing. Were they trying to talk to her?

Gail wanted to run, she didn't want to hear what they had to say and she feared they may break out of the wall and consume her. Yet with the pain and nausea, she was too weak to move, so all she could do was stand and stare.

Then the wall flattened, and the faces were all gone. She breathed a sigh of relief, maybe it was just the tumor. Maybe she's hallucinating again. Slowly, she reached out to touch the wall and just before she did one large face formed in the middle of it. The eyes opened and they were human eyes, blue eyes, bloodshot and weary, but definitely human. They seemed to look at her, and the mouth below them opened.

"Get him out of here or die."

At last her legs were free, and she ran out of the kitchen and into the hallway. As she tore across the room, she didn't notice that the tripods, cameras, meters and equipment had all gone. The house looked as it did when they arrived, empty, desolate, and untouched for many years. Gail ran as fast as she could in the semi-darkness hardly looking where she was going. Pulling up suddenly she reached out for the door handle, and the door was gone. With her heart in her throat, she looked around the room. All the doors had gone, there were just blank walls and an opening to the stairs.

Even the kitchen door, the one that she had just run from, was no longer there.

Chapter Twelve

Gail spun on the spot, around and around as the light chased shadows across the wall. What was happening? What was going on? As her head throbbed and her heart pounded against her ribs, she could make no sense of what she was seeing. The doors had all gone! There was no escape!

That was when she noticed the equipment was also missing. Was she hallucinating this, was it all in her mind? She took her left hand and squeezing through the thick fleece on her right arm she pinched as hard as she could. It hurt, and yet nothing changed. If this was a dream, then she was not waking up.

Again she turned a circle, the light chasing away the shadows and yet they reached in with their dark and cold fingers the moment it had passed. The light was ethereal and the darkness that chased it was menacing. In her mind, the dark was reaching out to take her. Where she did not know, yet she knew it was somewhere she did not want to go.

Jesse, she had to find Jesse, he was her only hope. Then she realized the staircase was her only exit. She was being herded upstairs, and suddenly, she remembered the window. So many deaths had happened from that window, would hers soon add to the list?

Fear held her back, and fear drove her onward. Again, she circled on the spot, not knowing what she should do.

Whispers surrounded her once more, and she spun to try and find the source. There was a smoky substance in the room, it floated just beyond her reach, and as the light hit it, it seemed to dissipate.

"Get away from me," she screamed. "Just leave me alone."

The whispering rose like a wave coming to a crescendo it crashed all around her. Gradually the words were becoming clearer... the voice was taunting her.

"Coward... Betrayer... Liar... Death."

The Haunting of Seafield House

The words were coming faster and faster, the same few over and over again and others she could not quite make out. There was a presence in the room. The smoke would form into the rough shape of a person and then it would dissipate before her very eyes. Occasionally she could feel things, hands touching her arms, her hair, and her back. One grabbed onto the jacket on her arm, and she yanked herself away, watching as the smoky figure disintegrated before her eyes.

It was too much, she had to find Jesse, so she bit down her fear and raced for the stairs.

"Jesse, help me please, wherever you are, Jesse, please, I need you now," she shouted the words as she ran up the stairs. There was no reply, just the sound of her footsteps strangely hollow on the creaky old steps. When she got to the top, she could see a faint light to the right, so she turned that way. A wave of relief passed over her for she was moving away from that dreadful room. The room with the window, the room of the suicides, the hands in the wardrobe and the murders.

There was a sliver of light under the door of the first room. Gail grabbed the handle, pushed it open, and burst inside. Relief flooded through her like hot chocolate on a cold night. Stood in the center of the room was Jesse, seeing him she knew that now she was safe.

"Jesse, Jesse, oh, my God, I found you. You won't believe what I've seen, we have to get out of here, we have to get out of here now." She ran towards him, the words streaming out of her in an incoherent babble.

Jesse stepped back and raised his right arm. Gail was so delighted to see him that she did not notice the knife held in it. Just before she could throw herself into his arms and onto that knife, Jesse stopped her.

"You cheated on me, you bitch," he swore at her.

It was such a shock, he never raised his voice, and he never swore. It brought her up sharp, and suddenly she saw the knife.

"What are you doing?" she begged of him, and as she did, she could hear laughing. It was Sarah, the cold, hard sound was unmistakable, and somehow she knew Sarah was behind all of this.

Jesse stepped towards her, slashing the knife before him and calling her a betrayer, a cheat, and a whore. Slowly, she backed away from him, watching the knife and his face. Looking for any sign of the man she loved, for any sign of recognition. There was none. For a moment, she thought about running and hiding. But where would she go? He had the only key to the house, without him there was no escape, and if she left him here at the mercy of this evil spirit she would never forgive herself.

So, she stood her ground and shouted back, "this is not you, Jesse, something is controlling you."

There was nothing, he didn't even slow down, and she noticed his gray eyes were darker. Cold, just like those of the girl. "Please give him back to me," she mumbled and then she tried to look into his eyes. To see past the hatred to the good man that lived there. "I love you, Jesse, and I know you love me, fight this. I think it's that girl, somehow, I think she's been here every time there's been a death. There is something evil about her, and she is controlling you. She's telling you things, but you can fight them. Remember last Christmas, when you found that picture... the one I had lost? You had it framed and gave it to me, and I was so happy, so grateful. Remember how much we love each other."

Gail was slowly backing away, frightened that with each step she would trip or run into something else. What if Sarah was behind her?

Jesse never faltered, never blinked, he just kept waving that knife with a sick expression on his face. Every now and then she thought she saw him flinch. She thought that maybe the real man surfaced for an instant, but whatever spell he was under, it was just too strong for him.

"Please, remember our time together," she pleaded. The only answer was a fierce growl as Jesse launched himself at her.

Gail jumped to the side and avoided the knife, but she knew it was time to run, she turned quickly, and he slashed at her. The knife sliced through her fleece and drew blood on her left arm. It was like being cut with ice, the whole arm was instantly numb. Again she turned, twisting to try and avoid him but Jesse was too fast and too strong. A strong hand grabbed hold of her arm and threw her to the ground, twisting her over until he kneeled above her.

"You cheated on me, you betrayed me, and for that, you die," he almost spat the words at her and Gail flinched at every one.

"You don't believe that... you know me," was all she could say.

Jesse raised the knife, the room was almost black, and yet it caught the light and seemed to dazzle her with its brilliance. With a manic grin on his face, he drew it to one side over her neck, and she knew he was going to slit her throat. That soon she would be dead. Anger overtook her fear, she had so little time, and yet this was not the way she wanted to die.

"Just go ahead," she shouted at him.

Jesse's eyes opened a little, and he eased back, holding the knife still poised above her throat.

"Go on," she screamed. "I'll be dead in six months anyway. I have a brain tumor, it's big, it's aggressive, and its terminal. So, go on and kill me... save me the pain and indignity that is to come."

Jesse's eyes seemed to clear. They lightened back to their normal gray, and he dropped the knife.

Gail let out a gasp as it rattled on the wooden floor.

Jesse got off of her and looked down at his hands.

"Gail, I... I... I don't know what happened. Please, forgive me. I don't want to lose you... I love you so much, and I can't believe that I might lose you. We will find something we can do, there must be something to cure you."

Reaching down he pulled her to her feet and into his arms. For long moments they hugged and gained confidence, warmth, and support from each other. Gail could feel tears running down her face. He was so sweet, and she knew it would hit him hard, but for now, she had to forget her tumor. For now, all that mattered was that they get out of the house alive. She pulled away.

"I know you don't want to hear this, but we cannot think about me now... that is for another day, and we have to leave."

Jesse nodded, there were tears in his eyes, and his cheeks glistened. "I have to do something," he said.

"Then get me out of here."

Grabbing her hand, he picked up the lantern and started toward the door. "I will, I promise... I just wish I could understand."

"It's the girl," Gail said. "Sarah, she is growing stronger, healthier and she said things. I think she has been here for all the deaths. I think she may be the reason for them. That she causes them somehow." Gail told him everything she had found out from Sarah.

"It makes sense," Jesse said. "If she was killed first then saw her mother killed then it could send her spirit mad. Now all she has is vengeance, and she is taking it out on anyone who comes here."

"Can we leave?"

Jesse nodded. "I want to find out more, but I can do that in the daylight. Come on, let's go."

He took her hand and led her to the door. As he did, he felt an intense surge of jealousy and found he was squeezing her fingers.

Gail winced and gasped.

"Sorry," he said.

"I know this is your dream," she said. "But you can research in the daylight, maybe it will be enough."

"It will be, I want to write a book on this house. Who knows, it could be a new career." He let out a sigh and stopped her for a moment. "I can't help the feelings I'm having. The spirit had given me an intense jealousy and built a rage inside me. It is hard to control. I imagine that is what happened to the other men. They were controlled and driven to a wrath that they could not understand or control."

"Great," Gail said and then winked. "Let's make this quick."

As they got to the door, a ghostly figure appeared before them.

Caroline Clark

Chapter Thirteen

Gail wanted to scream, but the sound would not get past the lump in her throat. She stopped instantly, and Jesse bumped her from behind.

The apparition was in the shape of a woman, though she was translucent and shimmered in the doorway. Long dark hair hung down over an elaborately embroidered blue dress that was covered in blood. As she morphed in and out of the shadows, they could see her face was beaten, bruised and bloody.

Though she made no noise her mouth opened and closed and each time it did the air in the room seemed to charge with static.

"Get behind me," Jesse said, and he moved around in front of her.

As she watched, he pulled a bottle from his pocket and the crucifix from his neck. Holding the crucifix out towards the phantom he screwed off the bottle top and splashed water on the apparition.

Gail knew it was holy water. There were many times when she had got annoyed as he was filling up the flask. He never let it stand for more than three months, and they made many trips to the local church. How she had resented them and yet now... she never believed that it would be useful and yet tonight it may save their lives.

For a moment she felt hope, maybe they could get out of this house and maybe she would have a few good months left. Only, the woman was becoming clearer before their very eyes. When she first appeared, she was just a blur, a movement on the air. As she formed, they could see through her completely and easily. Though she was not yet solid, she was more so, and the air was becoming more and more charged with menace.

"We drive you from us, whoever you may be, unclean spirits, all satanic powers, all wicked legions," Jesse chanted at the woman.

The Haunting of Seafield House

It seemed to be having no effect, and she came into the room as if she owned it, floating towards them as if she were entering a ballroom.

Slowly, she circled them as Jesse continued to chant. Still, her mouth opened and closed, and she brought with her a coldness that chilled to the bone.

"In the Name of Our Lord, Jesus Christ," Jesse chanted. "May you be snatched away and driven from the Church of God and from the souls made to the image and likeness of God and redeemed by the Precious Blood of the Divine Lamb."

She was moving closer to them and gaining strength. It was as if she blinked in and out of existence and each time she came back she was a little bit closer to reality, to being a corporeal body. Gail's heart was pounding, her knees were weak, and her hands were slick with sweat.

The spirit just kept coming no matter what Jesse did. Standing before her he did not look afraid. A flush of pride raised her hopes as she watched him chanting and throwing his holy water. Jesse never faltered, and yet she worked around behind them, and they had to back away to the door.

"She's heading us towards that window," Gail said.

Jesse nodded. "She's feeding on our fear and emotions. You have to fight the fear, I must fight my fear, rage, and jealousy. It is these emotions that are making her strong, that are bringing her onto this plane. By denying her these, we will have more chance of fighting her." For a second, he turned and found Gail's eyes. That look strengthened her, and she knew that he would keep her safe. "We must stick together," he said.

Gail took his hand and squeezed it before reaching up and kissing his cheek. "You are the only man for me, know that with all your heart."

Jesse kissed her back before turning and continuing his exorcism.

"Christ, God's Word made flesh, commands you. Be gone, Satan, inventor, and master of all deceit, the enemy of man's salvation. Unclean and evil beast, hear the Lord's words and be gone."

The woman was almost corporeal now, and they could hear more and more of the words she was mouthing.

"Deceiver... Betrayer... Liar. Give in and rest now. Let me show you the way to eternity," the words were so persuasive.

Gail wanted to listen, she wanted to believe them, and she had to shake herself to not fall under their spell.

Gradually, the spirit pushed them out of the room and along the corridor. Every step was like a nightmare that she wanted to escape from. She did not know how much more her heart could take and yet for the moment the pain had gone from her head. Maybe it was the adrenaline surging through her veins maybe it was just plain old fear. She did not know, and she did not care, she had to think of a way to help Jesse. Maybe if she prayed? So she did, she prayed and stepped back inch by tiny inch making sure that she kept away from the spirit. All the time she wondered why Jesse didn't just turn and run. Soon they would be at the stairs, and they could run down and escape.

"Where is the key?" she asked.

Jesse kept chanting, but he reached into his pocket and handed her the key as they slowly backed away down the corridor. The stronger the woman got, the less light the lantern gave out, and the colder the house seemed to become. If they tripped, then it was over, and so they inched back step by careful step giving up as little ground as they could.

Gail felt her hopes rising as they moved towards the stairs. There was no way the woman could stop them bolting down them, and once they did, they would be out the door. She didn't dare to think what would happen if it wasn't there. She hadn't mentioned that to Jesse, so she pushed it to the back of her mind. With each step, her legs felt weaker, and she was breathing so fast she feared she would hyperventilate and faint.

Jesse put a hand on her arm.

"Control the fear," he said, and she could see him gritting his teeth, his face was red, and his eyes were darker than they should be.

"I can't."

She wanted to mention the door, wanted to tell him there was no way out and yet that way was terror. So, she bit down on her lip and took a deep breath. Letting it out really slowly she managed to think of just the next step. That's all she had to do, just think of one second at a time. Every second they survived was one more victory, and they could beat this woman... this ghost. As she controlled her breathing the woman before her shimmered and was gone for just a second. It was a small victory, but it was a victory, and she took another breath, clearing her mind and just concentrating on her feet. Grabbing Jesse's arm, she hurried them back down the corridor, and they arrived at the stairs. As they turned the seed of hope was destroyed.

Standing three steps down was Sarah, her arms folded across her chest and an evil smile on her face.

The woman was back, the grin on her face one of victory. She moved closer to them, but Gail decided she had had enough. Taking Jesse's hands, she pulled him around to face her.

"This is where we make a stand," she said.

Jesse nodded and they linked arms and faced her. "We're going no further, do what you will."

Caroline Clark

Chapter Fourteen

As they held hands, Jesse continued to chant. "I cast you out, unclean spirit; in the name of our Lord, Jesus Christ, be gone from these creatures of God."

A laugh sliced through the air as effectively as a knife. It was deep and thick with phlegm, and it blasted them with more cold air. "You will die, you cannot defy me. It does not matter where this happens," she hissed. "Die as all who come within my house must die."

The house began to shudder, almost as if it was being shaken by an earthquake. Gail screamed, and Jesse pulled her close and yet he never stopped chanting.

Why wasn't it working?

Beneath them, the floorboards moved. It was as if they were made of rubber, the wood rose up, and they rushed backward, trying to race the undulating floor. Somehow, they knew that staying still meant death and yet there was nowhere to run. Back and back they went until they had a choice. Enter the room, the room with the window of death or run into the outside wall.

Without even a word they went past the door and stopped only when their backs were against the wall. Jesse pulled her to him and held her close, kissing the top of her head as they felt the floor boards move beneath their feet. At first, they were lifted up, but then the boards seemed to crumble away from them and shattered into a million pieces. For the briefest of instants, they were standing on nothing.

Gail felt her stomach fall as well as her feet and she was plummeting down, and down. Jesse was trying to hold on to her, but it was no use. He was heavier, and they tumbled apart. A scream was ripped from her as her hand reached out to grab him. Only, he was falling faster, and then there was a great crash, and he disappeared through the next floor. She screamed his name, afraid that he would be dead. Maybe it didn't matter, maybe she would join him soon.

As she passed through the next floor, she felt debris hit her face and scratch down her right arm. Then she was falling in pitch darkness, the lantern tumbling away before her. Automatically her arms wheeled, and her legs ran in the air and then she hit the floor.

Landing hard on her back, the air was forced from her lungs in a great whoosh and pain seared through her body. She was engulfed in a great cloud of dust. It was so dark, and yet the lantern had landed not far away from her. Something was blocking the light. A cough escaped her battered lungs, and for a few moments, she could not move. Every part of her hurt and tears leaked from her eyes. Though she desperately wanted to look for Jesse, to call his name, she could not move, could not even speak.

Closing her eyes, she tried to take a deep breath. It hurt in her chest and back. Was something broken? *Did it matter?* Shaking off such negative thoughts she took another, shallower breath. This one was less excruciating, and she could feel the pain receding and sensation coming back into her arms and legs. They hurt, she would no doubt be covered in bruises, but it looked like she would survive... for a little while anyway!

With great trepidation, she tried to sit up. A gasp of pain left her, but she made it.

"Jesse," she called softly.

The cellar was so dark, she needed to get to the lantern and to find Jesse. Could he have survived? It seemed doubtful. He had hit the second floor and had fallen through it. She had been lucky and had only gone through the hole. Yet she could feel blood on her arm and cheek. Carefully, she checked her arm. The blood was flowing, but not fast, she would survive. Then she gingerly touched her cheek. It hurt like hell, but the blood had stopped.

Gradually, her eyes were adjusting to the dark, and she looked around as she felt a cold breeze rush past her. It seemed to freeze her very soul, and she knew the spirits were here.

"Jesse, oh, my God, Jesse, we have to get out of here."

Gail scanned the room and then she saw him. He was lying between her and the lamp. He was not moving.

Gail tried to stand as she peered into the darkness. Her legs would not hold her, she still felt too dizzy, so she dragged herself across the dirt floor. All the time she could feel her panic rising, and she was making small choking sounds as she tried to hold it together.

What if he was dead?

At last, she was at his side, and she reached out a hand to touch him. He was warm but did

The Haunting of Seafield House

not move. The lantern was on the other side of him, and she reached over to grab it. It was almost too far, but she stretched, feeling a stabbing pain in her ribs. It was too far, and she started to sob. This was it, she would die in this cellar with Jesse. For a moment, she thought about lying down next to him and giving in. Then she felt angry. She had never given in to anything, and she was not starting now. So, she scrambled to her knees. Ignoring the pain that wanted her to scream, she reached over and grabbed the lantern.

Taking a breath and steadying herself, she looked at Jesse. He had a gash on his forehead. It was deep but not bleeding, and it was starting to bruise. That had to be a good sign, right? He could not bruise if he was dead. He looked so pale, but that could be the light, and she could not see if he was breathing.

Gently, she reached for his neck and as her fingers prodded his skin his eyes opened. The pupils dilated and then focused, and she wanted to let out a whoop of joy.

"Jesse," she said and hugged him close.

"Where are we?" he tried to sit up but his eyes closed and he sank back down.

"Steady now, you had a bad fall. We fell from the top floor, and you hit all the debris." She did not know how to describe what had happened. Would probably never know but she knew he must take his time… and yet she also knew they must hurry.

"Are we alone?" he asked.

Gail held the lamp up and looked around the cellar, it did not reach all that far but from what she could see they were. "I think so." Though she knew the spirits were here, they had not manifested yet.

"I think so, but I think they are coming. What should I do?" She wanted to cry, to tell him how frightened she was, how much she loved him and how she did not want him to die. Yet somehow, she knew that would just make things worse. Despite the terror in her stomach and the way her hands were shaking, she must appear to be calm.

Jesse took her hand. "You have to be strong. It will weaken them… that is why they are not here straight away. We stood up to them, and it has sent them back, but it will not hold. Listen to me, for this is very important."

Gail squeezed his hand. "I'm listening."

"Gail, my love, you have to leave. Go now and do not look back."

Gail felt as if the floor had collapsed once more. She could not leave him here, could not abandon him to those evil ghosts, spirits, apparitions or whatever they were. If she died it did not matter, but not Jesse, he had his whole life ahead of him, and she would not leave.

"No," was all she could say.

"You always were so darn pig-headed," he said, but there was a laugh in his voice. Only it ended in a coughing fit, and as he pulled his hand away, Gail could see blood on his fingers.

"Jesse!" she yelled. "How badly are you hurt?"

For a moment, she could see he was going to lie, but then he shook his head. "I think I broke a rib, possibly my ankle but I will survive. We just need to be strong and beat these bitches, and we will get out of here. Together," he said.

"Together."

"Can you help me move to the wall, to sit up?" he asked.

Gail wanted to say no, she wanted to keep him still but she could see it was a better position. They would be able to see the rest of the cellar from there.

"I'll try, can you stand?"

"For maybe a few paces."

Gail lifted, and Jesse pushed down on his arms and levered up onto one leg. His right ankle hung at a strange angle, and it almost made Gail wretch. Together, she helped as he hopped to the wall. When she put him down, she could see he was almost white and looked as if he would faint at any moment. Gently, she slapped his cheeks.

"Stay with me," she said.

"I'm OK. I just need a moment."

Only they didn't have a moment for the spirit of Sarah, and the woman flashed into view.

"Be strong," Jesse said, though his voice was weak and she could see he was fading. "The stronger you are, the weaker they will be." Then he took her hand. The gesture comforted her, made her think of home. It gave her strength and yet she could tell that his grasp was weak.

"I want to ask you to do something for me," Jesse said. "I need you to leave, I need you to leave me and to get out of here and then I will be happy."

"No!" Gail wailed. "There is no way I could leave you, no way I will."

The Haunting of Seafield House

"Please, please, just save yourself. This was my foolish dream... I need you to go." His voice faded away and as she watched his eyes closed.

Gail let out a sob and reached over to feel for his pulse. At first, she could not find it and tears formed in her eyes. Then there it was, weak, weak but steady. What should she do? She wanted to shake him, to slap him, anything to wake him up. Wasn't that what you were supposed to do? It was all too much, and she let the tears fall until she heard the mocking laughter of the child, Sarah.

There was something about that sound that incensed her. Fear wanted to bury her beneath a blanket of terror, but she would not let it. *What did it matter?* She was dead in a few months anyway, and so she would fight these bitches, and she would win. Raising her eyes, she looked at them.

They weren't fully corporeal but were more like shining figures of dark mist and yet the sight of them almost broke her resolve. The woman stood behind Sarah, her hands were on the child's shoulders. Gail looked closer and she could see bone poking through the skin and for some reason that gave her hope.

"You're not getting him, and if you know what's good for you, you will get out of here and leave us alone." She said the words with conviction and yet she did not know what else to do. The exorcism hadn't seemed to be working, and she was not sure she could remember it anyway. So, what could she do except be strong and stay with Jesse?

The ghost before her seemed to shimmer, it was as if her defiance weakened them and that gave her strength. So, she thought back through all the years, and all she had heard from Jesse and something came to her. The exorcism had to be complete before it could work and that the spirit would try to stop you doing that. This was what must be happening. She didn't know the exorcism, but she knew some of the words and she remembered hearing Jesse say that intent was as important as the words.

Getting to her feet, she walked towards the ghosts, and she started to chant, "Be gone, unclean spirit... be gone. I cast you out in the name of the Father, the Son, and the Holy Spirit. Be gone."

Sarah screamed, and the woman blinked out of existence for just a moment. When she returned the smile on her face was softer somehow, and she nodded as if in encouragement. Gail found herself staring at the woman. Their eyes met, and suddenly she was no longer as afraid. Was it because she did not fear death, or had something changed?

As she held the woman's glance, a dark mist traveled past her, and she turned to see Sarah in front of Jesse.

"No!" she screamed and rushed to him. It was too late.

Sarah picked Jesse up and tossed him across the cellar as if he was a ragdoll. He traveled beyond the scope of the light, and she heard a terrible crunch as he hit the wall. Picking up the lantern she raced towards him. Jesse was lying on the ground in front of the wall. Bricks had broken loose, and a few were scattered on top of him. Dropping to her knees, she grabbed the bricks and tossed them away. Fury gave her strength, and soon he was clear. Gently, she wiped the dust and dirt from his face.

"Jesse, Jesse, are you still... Jesse, please don't leave me, I beg you, don't go."

Her hand was shaking as she reached down to his neck, it hesitated just a few centimeters above his flesh. What would she do if he was dead? Nothing would matter anymore... but she would get her revenge. She would end this in the name of her love. Swallowing, she placed her fingers on his neck and searched for his pulse. A sob escaped her because she couldn't find it, it was almost too much, and she felt filled with fury. No, she had to stay strong, so she took in a deep breath and tried again.

Yes, it was there, very weak, but it was there. She had to get him out of here. Closing her eyes, she focused her rage and let it build within her. Then she stood and picked up the lantern, and something caught her eye. Raising the lantern to shoulder height she noticed a hole in the wall where Jesse had hit. That shouldn't have happened, the house was old but no way should he have knocked through the wall. With her heart in her mouth, she approached the dark gap. Could he have knocked clear through to the outside? Did they have a way to escape? Quickly, she scrambled over to the hole. Even though she knew it was impossible, so many impossible things had happened this night that she would believe in anything and she would take the hope. Maybe she could smash out some more bricks and drag Jesse out, maybe they would be safe?

Disappointment weighed on her like an anvil on her back. It was not to the outside. It was a cavern, a cubby, something that had been created inside the house. Slowly, she leaned forward. Every fiber of her was ready to move. Was this a trap? Had Sarah done this deliberately? Maybe she would be dragged into that hole and sealed inside. Though it was the last thing she wanted to do, she peered inside.

"No!"

Gail could not help but scream.

Chapter Fifteen

Staring back at her from behind the bricks were the empty eye sockets of a skeleton. Gail's knees started to buckle, and the breath froze in her throat. Quickly, she had to grab onto the wall to steady herself, and a brick came away in her hands. It landed on her foot and sent needle sharp pain through her toe. The pain focused her mind, and she steadied herself and forced her eyes back to the skeleton.

Its mouth was open in a silent scream. Had this woman been put here, still alive? Was this what would happen to her? To her and Jesse?

For what seemed like minutes, and yet could only have been seconds Gail just stood there and stared. Her mind could not comprehend what she was seeing. The ghost of the woman appeared beside her, and she seemed more real, almost human. Gail felt tears fill her eyes as she looked from the ghost to the skeleton trapped in the wall. Though there were little of the clothes left on the bones, the color of the material could be the same. Gail let out a sob. Had this woman been sealed in this wall alive?

The ghost raised her hands, and Gail was overcome with fear and nausea. The fingernails were broken, the ends of the fingers scratched and bleeding. The skin was worn almost down to the bone.

"You were buried alive?" Gail asked.

The spirit nodded.

"You did this to your hands?"

The spirit nodded once more.

Tears were streaming down Gail's face as she imagined the horror and fear the woman must have suffered. Sealed in a dark tomb, scratching at the bricks with your fingers until you ripped off your own nails and all the skin. How long had she clawed against that impenetrable fortress and yet there was no escape? The panic must have been unbearable, and how long had it taken for her to die? Hours, days? It did not bear thinking about. Trapped in the dark, was her greatest fear... but to be trapped with no hope and no chance of salvation? Had she starved to death? Or died of lack of oxygen? Or maybe her heart gave out under the sheer terror. However she had died, she had died alone and afraid, and suddenly, Gail felt sorry for her.

"I'm sorry," Gail said.

A scream of anger echoed across the cellar and Gail was hit from behind and knocked to the ground. A feeling of cold and pain seared across her muscles and yet she knew she could not give in. Quickly, she rolled onto her back and scooted along the wall. Stood in front of her was Sarah. Though she could not hear anything, Gail could see she was shouting at the woman. Then the two spirits seemed to mingle. It looked like the woman was fighting. Sarah's form was forced away from her and back towards the hole in the wall. Hands appeared from the dark. They flexed and reached and grasped, and they took hold of Sarah and held her tight.

The cellar was full of whispers. A hundred voices, all talking at once surrounded Gail. Fighting down her fear she tried to concentrate. Yet her eyes were drawn to the hands holding onto the ghost of Sarah. The girl was furious and fighting hard, it was obvious they would not hold for long. Gail had to do something, and she had to do it now.

"I can't hear you. Talk one at a time," she called into the darkness.

The whispers rose and thickened, as if angry, and then they faded away until just one voice spoke.

"There are ten of us here. Ten souls, ten of us trapped by this wicked girl. Help us, save us. I beg of you, give us peace."

"I will," Gail said. "But you must help me. We must get Jesse out of here alive."

The whispers rustled like leaves and Gail believed they were consulting.

"We will do what we can, but she is strong, you must be stronger."

The figure of the woman flickered, it was as if the talking had taken all her strength. She was fading, becoming more and more translucent and then she was gone. At that very instant Sarah escaped from the hands. A sneer formed on her face and she charged at Gail.

Gail felt her knees go weak, her stomach tense. How could she fight this? How could she survive this? Then she looked down at Jesse, and she knew she had to. So, she waited, and just as the child got to her, she stepped to one side. The ghost whooshed past her in a blast of cold air, but Sarah turned so quickly. Much quicker than Gail could, and hands of ice hit her back so hard, she was pushed into the ground.

For a moment, Gail was stunned. She could feel the figure on her back, could feel it forcing her head into the ground and terror started to take over. Would she die in this cellar choking on the dust?

Then a voice appeared in her head.

"You must be strong, Gail," it was Jesse's voice from earlier, and it boosted her.

Gail gathered all her strength and rolled her hip. The child was flung from her, and she managed to roll over onto her back gasping desperately for breath. Yet, before she could stand Sarah was back on top of her.

The cold weight on her chest seem to be compressing her lungs, and she found she could not breathe. It was as if her lungs were frozen and could not move enough to draw in even a bit of air.

Sarah sat atop of her, a look of glee on her face.

"Give in," Sarah whispered inside Gail's mind. "I am in control, and you are going to die, why make it hard?"

For a moment, Gail wanted to do as she was told. It was as if she had no energy and no fight left. She felt drained by the cold and just as she was about to let go, to succumb to the peace of death, her eyes saw Jesse. He was still not moving, maybe he was already dead. It didn't matter, she would not give up on him as he would never give up on her.

"I'm not afraid of you, and you will never win. Not this time, you evil bitch. So, back off from me or die, the choice is yours."

The pressure on Gail's chest eased just a little. Maybe this was working, maybe this would be her way of exorcising the spirit. It didn't matter, it felt good to take back control even if only for a little bit.

Sarah drew back her hand and slapped Gail across the face. She could feel the bones beneath the fingers. They were like shards of ice and sliced into her cheek. She could not let her do it again as she did not think her body could take much more. The pain in her head had returned with the slap, and she felt as if the tumor was squeezing her brain. It made her dizzy, and she knew she did not have long. Once more, she rolled her hip only this time Sarah was ready, and the child tilted to the side and was not unseated.

Was this it? Was there nothing more she could do?

No, she would go down fighting and if words were all she had to fight with, then that was all she would use.

"Leave here, you evil, unclean spirit. Be gone, for I cast you out in the name of Jesus Christ, our Savior. No one wants you here, you rotten, evil, spawn of Satan, be gone for I am not afraid of you."

Sarah started to flicker, and the weight on Gail's chest was much less.

"I cast you out, you spawn of Satan," Gail chanted as she rolled her left hip this time and tipped the spirit from her body.

It was like a block of ice had been lifted from her, and she was filled with energy. Her lungs gratefully took in a gasp of air. Taking no time, she stood up and moved towards the hole in the wall. The ghost of the woman appeared again, and lots of hands were showing over the bricks.

There must be more bodies behind there?

Gail pushed the thought out of her mind. That was something for another day. Today she had this battle to fight, and she was going to win it. For some reason, she reached out and took hold of the ghost woman's hand. At first, there was nothing beneath her fingers, but as she began to chant and shout at Sarah, she could feel flesh developing there. Part of her knew it should be gross and yet it gave her strength. She continued to shout and wail at Sarah, not knowing what she said or whether it would work. It didn't matter, it gave her strength.

Then she noticed the sound of Latin in the air. It was a sweet, clear voice and she turned to see the woman talking. Soon other voices added to the chorus.

"Be gone, you foul-smelling, rotten, evil spirit," Gail continued to chant. Part of her wanted to laugh at the words she was using, but then she remembered *it's all about intent* and she poured her soul and heart into the words. Imbuing the words with her meaning. The intention of forcing this ghost from this house and from these other spirits.

Suddenly, there was another woman to her right. Gail felt another hand on hers, and she squeezed it gently. Together they would face this, and together they would win.

"I cast you out, evil spirit, I cast you out in the name of the Lord, and I claim this place as a place of peace. Be gone, for you are not welcome here and we do not fear you."

Sarah let out a scream and seemed to fade before them.

The Haunting of Seafield House

"No one fears you anymore. We think you are nothing. Evil is nothing, and it is not welcome here. Be gone, unclean spirit, be gone and never return."

Before her eyes, Sarah's face distorted. It transformed through a myriad of emotions. There was fear, anger, and fury, but with each emotion, she was getting weaker, fainter. As Gail continued to shout her nonsense exorcism, Sarah dissolved into nothing.

Once she was gone the cellar seemed lighter, and Gail took in a sweet deep breath.

"Jesse will be all right," the woman's voice was inside Gail's head. "I have things to tell you, things I must ask you to do, and I apologize for my part in this. Will you help us?"

Gail nodded and blinked away tears. If Jesse was safe she could do anything... for however long she had left.

The woman put her hands on Gail's head, and for a moment she felt an intense pain. It was as if white light was searing through her brain and then she began to see images and understand things. It was as if she was living through other lives.

The woman's name was Jenny Thornton. She had moved here with her husband in 1900 after the death of her first child. Jenny had not been able to let the child go, and she would pretend it was still there. Sometimes, she saw this girl who she now knew was Sarah. At the time, she thought it was a blessing, the spirit of her dead child, and she spent all her time with her.

This incensed her husband, and his jealousy and rage grew. She knew it was her fault, that she was not paying him attention but she could not let go of the daughter she had lost and the new one she had gained.

What she now knew was that Sarah was the child of a woman who was the first occupant of the house. She had seen her mother murdered at that window and had killed her own father in a fit of anger. As her mother took her last breath, she cursed Sarah to walk the earth and exact revenge on all men. Jenny found out that Sarah could make men angry and jealous. That she played on those emotions and drove them mad.

One day, Jenny's husband broke under the spirits spell and threw her from the window.

Once more, Gail was falling, this time she knew it was not herself and yet the terror was every bit as bad. Down and down she tumbled until she hit the sharp rocks at the bottom of the window. Something broke inside of her, and the pain was so intense that she cried out. Then there was blackness.

The next thing she knew she was in a dark hole, and she was scraping against bricks. Overcome with terror she screamed and scraped until her nails were ripped off and her fingers were torn to the bone, but still, there was no escape. Eventually, exhaustion and her injuries overcame her, and she fell unconscious. She woke two more times before she finally died, each time she was more and more afraid. The dark was like a living beast that teased and taunted her. There were noises within it, and there was the fear of what came next. Would she meet her precious daughter or would she simply be gone... be nothing?

Gail had to bite down her own screams as she felt the fear and desperation, and then she was thrust into another home and another family. They were watching television, it was old and black-and-white, and they were dressed in clothes from a time long ago. Then she saw Sarah and another burst of fear went through her. Was this not over?

Gail could not control the visions, and soon she watched as the father beat a woman and Sarah seemed to look on with glee. Then the scene changed, and the telly showed the moon landing. It was 1969 if she remembered rightly and she had never seen it. How could that be? Something as momentous as the first time a man walked on the moon, and she had never seen it. Tears formed in her eyes and suddenly she wanted to watch that broadcast more than anything. She wanted to live, even if only for a few months.

She was part of an argument that developed, and she felt the fear of the victim as well as confusion as the husband was shouting at her. Then he hit her and then he was handed the knife by Sarah. The man was enraged, and he stabbed her over and over. Each blow filled her with excruciating pain, and she felt the fear and confusion of the victim and then the sadness just before she was dead.

Gail watched as the police arrived and they searched for the girl, but she could not be found. Then she saw Jenny as a spirit, hiding the child. Only Sarah escaped, and she cornered the man in the bedroom that Jenny had fallen from. The next thing Gail saw was Sarah pushing the man from the window. As soon as he fell she blinked out of existence. Had she been a ghost even then? It looked like she had. It looked like she created havoc between whoever lived in this house and she fed on the fear and death that she caused.

Gail was shown more and more visions and each time the same thing happened. There were a couple who were dared to stay a night in the house. Just like her and Jesse, they came across the girl and tried to look after her. They were both killed, the woman murdered by the man and he was pushed from the window. The bodies were never found. Time after time Gail lived the horror that happened to these people. As she did, she got to know them. She knew their relatives, knew who to tell and she promised each and every one of them that she would see that they were put to rest and that she would let their relatives know.

After the last vision, Gail collapsed on the floor. She was exhausted. She managed to crawl over to Jesse and laid down next to him. Somehow, she knew she was safe now and so she let the sleep come.

Caroline Clark

Chapter Sixteen

Gail woke in the dark. She thought she heard voices and a burst of adrenaline raised the hairs on her arm. Was this not over? Then she heard the voices again.

"Gail, Jesse, where are you?" It was a man's voice this time, and she recognized it, but still, she could not place it.

There were sounds of somebody walking, and the light was getting closer. Though she ached and felt bruised and battered, she did not seem to be in a bad state. Slowly, she sat up. Where was Jesse?

"Jesse, Jesse, are you there?" She was feeling beside her, but the lamp seemed to have gone out in the night but at last her hands found Jesse. Someone was coming and as they walked the light flashed across Jesse's face, and she saw his eyes blink.

He was alive!

Joy filled her, and she reached out to hold his hand, for some reason she no longer feared what was to come. She had a few months left, and they would spend them together. For what time she had left, she would live. Then a light seared into her eyes, and she shut them tightly.

"Is that you? Gail, Jesse, is that you?"

This time she truly recognized the voice. It was Ben from the pub, and she could not be more pleased to see anyone. She had tears in her eyes, and she blinked them away not wanting him to see her as weak. Could she stand? Tentatively, she tried, and though she was stiff, she got to her feet.

"Yes, it's us," she managed as she walked towards him. "Jesse's hurt, I don't know how badly but we need help."

Ben was suddenly in front of her, and he pulled her into his arms.

"You did it, you survived a night in Seacliff house. That is really something, in fact, I never thought I'd see the day. Most of the people, they think that no one died here. They think people just got bored and left, but I knew something was wrong. I came into this place before, and I could feel the evil. I swore I would never come back but you two... you two have made my day."

"Is help coming?" Gail asked as she pulled out of his arms.

"Not yet but I can make a call. Would it be all right to move Jesse? Can I carry him out of the house?"

Gail got back down on her knees and took Jesse's hand. He was awake and breathing easily.

"How are you?" she asked.

"My ankle hurts like hell, and so do a few other bits, but I feel better than last night. I'll survive... thanks to you. Some kind of spiritual investigator I turn out to be... saved by my girlfriend."

Gail laughed and pulled him into her arms and for a moment, she simply hugged him tightly.

"Ben's here, do you want to wait for the paramedics or he can get you out of here?"

"I just want to see the sunlight," Jesse said. "It's good to see you, Ben. I think you have the best pub in the country and I might even take you up on that room."

"The things I'll do for a compliment," Ben said as he stepped closer. As he moved the torch, he saw the hole in the wall and the skeleton in there.

"But, I'll be…" he said. "Is this the cause of our haunting?"

"Not exactly?" Gail looked at the skeleton, and she pitied the spirit left there. "This woman helped me."

"I sense a story coming on here?" Ben said, and then he swooped down and lifted Jesse easily from the floor. He handed Gail the torch.

"You lead the way, but be careful, there is a lot of debris."

Gail set out across the cellar floor. Now that the spirits were gone, that the house was at ease, it looked so much different. It was just a dilapidated old house. Still, she was glad to get upstairs and find that the door was where it should be. It looked like Ben had broken it down. Maybe that was what woke her. As she stepped out of the door and felt the sun on her face, she laughed and turned in a circle. It felt so good.

Ben placed Jesse sideways in the passenger seat of his Volvo. Then he went to one side and called an ambulance.

"You have to tell me all about it," Jesse said.

Part of Gail wanted to forget everything that had happened, but another part wanted to tell the story. If she had longer, maybe she would even write it all down, maybe she would even publish it. Only, she did not know how long she had and it was imperative that she talk to the relatives to see that they found peace. No, that was not the first thing she had to do. The first thing was to see that the bodies were laid to rest and that the spirits that had been trapped in this house were finally allowed to go... wherever they would go.

For now, she stood next to Jesse and held his hand and told him what had happened.

The story was just complete when the ambulance arrived. Jesse's eyes were huge, and she could see the excitement there, but there was one thing more that she had to say.

"You remember I told you I have a brain tumor. At times, when I was hearing things, seeing things, I thought I was hallucinating. Well, I don't have long to live, but I want to live to the fullest with whatever time I have left. There will be no more hospitals, no more talk of ghosts. I will honor my commitment to the spirits here, and then I want to enjoy the time I have. Can we do that?"

"Yes," Jesse said, and she could see tears running down his face.

She pulled him close and hugged him until the paramedics separated them.

***

They were taken to the hospital. Everyone seemed to be staring and whispering behind their hands, but they did not care. They had survived, and they were together. Both of them had injuries, he had a broken ankle, two broken ribs, a deep gash to his forehead and lots of other cuts and abrasions. The doctors said he would make a full recovery.

Gail had a broken rib and cuts and bruises, she needed a few stitches here and there but all in all, she was pleased with how little harm she had suffered. It could have been so much worse.

After they had been released from the hospital, Gail and Jesse returned to the house to find the police still there. The officers allowed them in and explained to them what they had found. In the cubby, in the cellar, they had discovered 11 adult skeletons and then they had found the skeleton of a young girl amongst the floorboards.

Gail spent some time with the officers telling them all she knew. Yet, she did not think they believed her, maybe they thought she was involved, but no one tried to keep her there. So, after all the bodies were found she gathered up Jesse's equipment, then loaded it in the car and they drove back to the pub.

Ben stood behind the bar, and he welcomed them as Jesse swung in on his crutches. Gail was walking behind him, a hand ready in case he fell.

"How are the conquering heroes?" Ben asked.

"We're doing fine, thanks to you and this wonderful woman here," Jesse said as he hauled himself onto a barstool. "However, we've had enough of ghost hunting for the next month or two." There was sadness on his face that Ben would not understand, so he bit down on his lip and forced a smile onto his lips. Gail was right, it was time to live.

Gail sat on a stool next to him and smiled at Ben.

"Thank you," she said.

Ben put down the glass he was polishing and leaned against the bar.

"I should be thanking the two of you, this story will keep me going for years." He winked at the two of them before picking up the glass again.

"It's late, and you to have a long drive home, why don't you take me up on the offer of that room?"

Gail and Jesse shared a look, and they both nodded. The last thing they could face was a long drive right now. So, they spent the next hour talking and eating before retiring to a beautiful room with a four-poster bed. Gail helped Jesse onto the bed and then took a long shower before she climbed in herself. Jesse was already asleep, so she leaned over and kissed his forehead before snuggling down. She had never felt anything quite so luxurious, and within minutes of pulling the covers over her shoulder, she was fast asleep.

Epilogue

Jesse held the door open for a smiling and laughing Gail. She walked in, and he could not believe how good she looked. They were both tanned having spent just under a month under the African sun. It had been a wonderful trip full of great memories, and he could not believe how well Gail had kept up with him. Before their visit to Seafield house, she had been tired. Now that he knew she was ill he recognized that she had been in a lot of pain, but now... she seemed so healthy and carefree.

They planned to be home for a few weeks before leaving for one last trip, this time to America and the Grand Canyon. After that, Gail had visited both of the places that she had always wanted to see. She had even watched an old recording of the moon landing, crying while he held her tight.

They had never been so close, and Jesse was both happy to have this time with her and sad that it would be cut so short. It felt such a cheat to get this wonderful time together knowing that soon she would be gone. That the tumor would eat away at her brain and leave her riddled with pain and only half the person that she was now. At times it made him so angry that he just wanted to scream and shout, but he would never do it when she could hear. No, that would be saved for after... how would he cope?

While Gail put the kettle on, he brought in the suitcases. He carried them upstairs and took them into the spare room where he saw all the equipment from the ghost hunt. So far, he hadn't looked at any of it. None of the recordings had been viewed or listened to, and suddenly, he wanted to see what he had captured. Though, there was one thing he wanted more. It was something they had argued about on the plane, but he was adamant, and eventually, Gail had agreed.

Tomorrow she was going to the hospital. Even though she had refused to let him go with her, she had at least agreed to go. So, tomorrow they would find out how long she had, and if they had time to make that final trip.

***

The Haunting of Seafield House

As soon as Gail left for the hospital, Jesse felt drawn to the spare room and his equipment. First, he went to the camcorder. He had plugged it in the night before, and the battery was now fully charged. It looked a bit battered and was very dirty but still, he hoped that it played. Though he no longer felt the same draw and excitement to investigate spirits he still wanted to know if anything had been recorded. Though he did not know what he would do if it had.

First, he wiped off all the dust and then plugged it into his laptop. The recordings were dark, and at times all he could hear was static but then the picture cleared. There were two faint shapes on the screen. He could not say they were people there were just shadows in the darkness. Then he heard them speaking, and the hairs on the back of his neck stood on end. It was Sarah and Jenny, and they were arguing.

"You are bound to me, your soul is mine," Sarah spoke on the recording. The voice was strong and challenging. Even sat here in the light and miles away from Seafield house he found it would have been hard not to do as she said. The next words chilled him to the bone.

"You will help me kill these two like we have killed all the ones before. All men are jealous, evil, and easily manipulated, and all women let you down. Let me bind them to me so they can help me for the rest of time."

The older voice was trying to argue, but it was obvious that she was under some form of control.

"There is no need to do this, let them go. Please, just this one time let them go."

The sound of Sarah's laughter set his nerves on edge.

"Do as I say, or your daughter will suffer," Sarah said.

Jesse watched more and more of the video. Most of it was blank, or just the two of them walking around. However, there was the odd snippet of conversation but nothing as detailed as that first exciting portion. Occasionally, he saw movement, a blur on the screen, you could not make out what it was. If he took this into the University would anyone believe him? If they hadn't been there, maybe they would just think it was a hoax. Maybe in a year or two, even he would think it was a hoax.

He checked his watch, it was the time that Gail would be in her appointment. How he hoped he could have been there, but he understood why she did not want him. If the news was bad, she would want the time to gain control. Gail had decided she would not feel

The Haunting of Seafield House

sorry for herself. That what time she had left was for living, and not for looking backward.

He was nearly at the end of the tape now, and he had seen a blur as he was thrown across the room. It was impossible to see who threw him or even that it was him. Yet that awful crunch when he hit the wall sent shivers down his spine. What happened after that he had only heard about for he was already unconscious and he listened in, eager to find out as much as he could.

Gail had told him what happened and yet seeing it here was almost unbelievable. The camera was on its side, and it was far enough away that he could see Gail, small and faint in the distance. At times he could see a blur that must be Sarah and another that must be Jenny. It all played out exactly as she said. More blurs appeared beside her, and he could hear the sound of chanting in Latin. Gail didn't know Latin, and there was more than one voice. Over it all, he could hear Gail trying to perform an exorcism. At times, he wanted to laugh; if you didn't know this was real, it would be very funny. And yet, it was real, and this brave woman had saved him by cursing at the spirits and telling them she would not give in.

As they continue to chant, he watched a blur that was Sarah dissolving into nothing and then the disturbance on Gail's right formed into a woman. She had long brown hair and was wearing a blue dress. It was too far away to see anything else, and yet he could hear her talking. Could hear her explain to Gail what to do to release the spirits and how to inform the families.

Then something happened that took his breath away.

She put her hands on Gail's head. Gail dropped to her knees, and the woman held her hands around her skull. White light seemed to surround Gail's head. Then he heard her talking, and he could not believe what he heard. So, he rewound the recording and listened again.

Jesse was breathless and feeling euphoric, could it be true?

Downstairs, the door opened, and he heard Gail rush in. She was laughing and talking so fast that he couldn't understand her. Pausing the recording, he ran from the room and downstairs.

Tears were streaming down her face, and he pulled her into his arms fearing the worst, fearing the recording was a lie.

"What is it?" he asked.

All Gail could do was laugh, and he found tears running down his own cheeks.

"Gail, what is it? Please tell me."

Gail pulled out of his arms and took his hands in hers.

"It's gone," she said.

"What's gone?" he asked, though he hoped he knew the answer.

"The tumor, the doctor says the tumor has gone and that I am healed. Jesse, I am healed, I am not going to die."

Jesse pulled her into his arms and kissed her head, cheeks, and lips. They were both crying, and he could taste the salty tears, but he did not mind, she was going to live.

"I have to show you something," he said some minutes later and led her up to the spare room.

Gail dug her heels in, she had been adamant that she did not want to see anything from the house or anything about ghosts, and yet here he was trying to show her the recordings.

"Trust me," Jesse said as he led her to a chair.

Then he played the recording. First, it was just static and light and dark moving on the screen. She saw what she thought was Sarah dissolve and she felt a huge sense of relief. It had really happened. Then she saw Jenny materialize and herself drop to her knees. Jenny put her hands on Gail's head, and she saw a white light that surrounded her head. A shiver ran down her spine, and she could feel her heart pounding. What was she going to see?

She could hear Jenny talking, but then the sound seemed to distort and slow down then as it sped up again the words become clear.

"Let me take this burden from you, let me take this pain," Jenny said.

Gail turned to Jesse and they were both crying. Could this really be true? Could Jenny have done this to her, could she have saved her life? They would never know for sure but in her heart she knew and she closed her eyes and gave Jenny her thanks. She thought she heard a whisper back.

"It is I who owe you. You released me and my daughter."

***

Never miss a book.

Subscribe to Caroline Clark's

newsletter for new release announcements and occasional free content:

http://eepurl.com/cGdNvX

Caroline Clark

Preview:

The Haunting of Brynlee House

25th April 15 82
The basement of the cage.
Derbyshire.
England.

3:15 am.

Alden Carter looked down at his shaking hands. The sight of blood curdled his stomach as it dripped onto the floor. For a moment, his resolve failed, he did not recognize the thin, gnarled fingers. Did not recognize the person he had become. How could he do this, how could he treat another human being in this terrible way and yet he knew he must. If he did not, then the consequences for him would be grave. For a second he imagined a young girl with a thin face and a long nose. Her brown hair bounced as she ran in circles and she flashed a smile each time she passed. The memory brought him joy and comfort. Brook was not a pretty girl, but she was his daughter, and he loved her more than he could say. He remembered her joy at the silver cross he gave her. The one that he was given from the Bishop, the one that cost him his soul.

Rubbing his hands through sparse hair, he almost gagged at the feeling of the crusty blood he found there. How many times had he run those blood-soaked fingers through his lank and greasy hair? Too many to count. It had been a long night, and it was not over yet. This must be done, and it was him who had to do it.

Suddenly, his throat was dry, and fatigue weighed him down like the black specter of death he had become. A candle flickered and cast a grotesque shadow across the wall. Outside, the trees shook their skeletal fingers against the brick and wood house and he closed his eyes for a moment. Seeing Brook once more he strengthened his resolve. The trees trembled, and the wind seemed to whisper through their leaves, tormenting him, telling him that he was wrong but he would not stop. Could not stop. Taking a breath, he felt stronger now, and with a shaky hand, he picked up an old stein and took a drink of bitter ale. It did not quench his thirst, but it gave him a little courage. He must do this. He must go back down to the cage and finish what he had started, for if he did not Brook would not survive and maybe neither would he?

The kitchen was sparse and dark and yet he knew he was lucky. The house was made of brick as well as wood. It was three stories' high and was bigger than he needed. This was a luxury few could afford. As was the plentiful supply of food in the pantry and work every day. The Bishop had been kind to him, and he knew he had much to be grateful for. Yet, what price had he paid? As the wind picked up, the trees got angry and seemed to curse him with their branches. Rattling against the walls and making ghostly shadows through the window. Alden turned from them and up to the wall before him. The sight of it almost stopped his heart and yet he knows he must go back down to the cage. If the Bishop found him up here with his job not done, then he would be in trouble... Brook would be in trouble. A shiver ran down his spine as he approached the secret door. Reaching out a shaky hand he touched the wall. It was cold, hard and yet it gave before him. With a push, the catch released and the door swung inward. Before him was a dark empty space. A chasm, an evil pit that he must descend into once more.

Picking up the oil lamp, he approached the stairs and slowly walked down into the dark. The walls were covered in whitewash, and yet they did not seem light. Nothing about this place seemed light. Shadows chased across the ceiling behind him and then raced in front as if eager to reach the hell below. Cobwebs clawed at his face. These did not bother Alden, he did not fear the spider, no, it was the serpent in God's clothing who terrified him.

With each step, the temperature dropped. He had never understood why it was so much colder down here. Cellars were always cool, but this one... with each step, he felt as if he was falling into the lake. That he had broken through the ice and was sinking into the water. Panic clenched his stomach as he wondered if he would drown. The air seemed to stagnate in his lungs, and they ached as he tried to pull in a breath. It was just panic, he shook it off, and was back on the stairs. His feet firm on the stone steps he descended deeper and deeper. He shrugged into his thick, coarse jacket. The material would not protect him, of that he was sure, but he pushed such thoughts to the back of his mind and stepped onto the soft soil of the basement floor.

There was an old wooden table to his right. Quickly, he put the oil lamp on it. Shadows chased across the room. In front of him, his work area was just touched with the light, he knew he must look confident as he approached the woman shackled to the wall. Ursula Kemp was once a beauty. With red hair and deep green eyes. Her smooth ivory skin was traced with freckles, and she had always worn a smile that had the local men bowing to her every need. Seven years ago she had married the blacksmith, and they had a daughter, Rose. Alden felt his eyes pulled to his right... there in the shadows lay a pile of bones. A small pile, the empty eyes of the skull accused him. Though he could not look away from that blackened, burned, mound... the cause of another stain on his soul. Bile rose in his throat, and the air seemed full of smoke. It was just his imagination, he swallowed, choked down a cough and pulled his eyes away. Blinking back tears, he turned and looked up at Ursula. Chained to the wall she should be beaten, broken, and yet there was defiance in her eyes. They were like a cool stream on a hot summer's day. Something about them defied the position she was in. How could she not be beaten? How could she not confess?

"Confess witch," he said the words with more force than he felt. Fear and anger fired his speech and maybe just a little shame. "Confess, and this will be over."

Ursula's eyes stared back at him cool, calm, unmoving. She looked across at the bones, and he expected her to break. Yet her face was calm… her lips twitched into a smile.

Alden's eyes followed hers. The bones were barely visible in the dark, but he could still see them as clear as day. A glint of something sparkled in the lamplight, but he did not see it. All he could see was the bones. Sweat formed on his palms as if his hands remembered putting them there. Remembered how they felt, strangely smooth and powdery beneath his fingers. *Ash is like silk on the fingers…* a sob almost escaped him, and for a second he wanted to free Ursula, to tell her to run… and yet, if he did then the Bishop may turn him and Brook into a heap of ash like the one he was trying to not look at.

In his mind, he heard the sound of a screaming child, the sound of the flames. Smelt the burning, an almost tantalizing scent of roasting meat. Shaking his head, he pushed the thoughts away. Now was the time for strength. Biting down on his lip, he fought back the tears and turned to face her once more.

"You will not break me," she shouted defiantly. "Unlike you, I have done no wrong. Kill me, and I will haunt you and your family until the end of time."

Alden turned as anger overrode his judgment, striding to the table he picked up a knife. It was thin, cruel, and the blade glinted in the lamplight. Controlling the shaking of his hands, he crossed the room and plunged it into her side. For a second it caught... stopped by the thickness of her skin. Controlled by rage, he leaned all his strength against it and it sliced into her. Slick, warm blood poured across his fingers. "Confess, confess NOW," he screamed spraying her face with spittle.

A noise from above set his heart beating at such a rate that he thought she must hear it. It pounded in his chest and reminded him of his favorite horse as it galloped across the fields.

The Bishop was here.

Without a confession, he was damned, but maybe he was damned anyway. Maybe his actions doomed him to never rest, yet he must save his daughter, he must save his darling Brook.

As he heard the door above open, panic filled his mind, he must act now, or it would be too late. Then he saw it in her eyes, Ursula knew what was coming. She knew she would die soon and yet she did not fear it. Maybe she thought she would meet her daughter, that they would be together again. He did not know, but the calm serenity in her eyes chilled him to the bone.

In a fit of rage, he struck her on the temple. The light left her eyes, her head dropped forward, and she was unconscious, but it no longer mattered… he had a plan.

"You have confessed," he shouted. "You are a witch. By the power of the church, I sentence you to death, you will be hung by the neck until you die."

Before the Bishop reached him, he pulled back his hand and slapped her hard across the face. The slap did not wake her, but the noise resounded across the cellar. As the Bishop stopped behind him, he felt an even deeper chill. This man had no morals, no conscience. Alden knew what he had done was wrong, but he did not care. If it kept his family safe, he would sacrifice any number of innocents, and yet his stomach turned at the thought of what was to come.

"You have your confession," the Bishop's voice was harsh in the darkness. "Let us hang her and end this terrible business."

***

The Haunting of Seafield House

Ursula woke to the feel of rough, coarse hemp around her neck. As her eyes came open, she felt the pain in her side and knew it was a mortal wound. The agony of it masked the multiple injuries she had received over the past few days.

Alden was holding her. Hoisting her up onto a platform which was suspended over the rail of the balcony. The rope tightened as he placed her feet on the smooth wood and fear filled her. This was it, she knew what was coming, and yet she shook the fear away. To her side, the Bishop stood, a lace handkerchief in his hand as he dabbed at the powder on his face. Blond hair covered a plump but handsome visage, with good bones and a wide mouth, but his eyes... they were gray and hard. The color of a gravestone they could cut through granite with just a look. Amusement danced in them, or maybe it was just the lamp flickering. It could not provide nearly enough for her to really tell, and yet she knew.

Alden moved away from her and turned to the Bishop. There was a hardness to him too. His lips were drawn tight enough to make a thin line, but he could not fool her. Alden was afraid, and she pitied him, pitied the days to come. For her, it was over. Death would be a sweet release, but for Alden, it had only just begun. As he pushed the table, she looked down to the floor below. The lamp did not light more than half way, and it seemed that she would jump into a bottomless pit. If the rope did not stop her... then maybe she could fly. Down deep she hoped she would soar, away from pain, away from fear and safe in the knowledge she held.

If only.

The moon came from behind a cloud and shone through the window at her back. Its light cast shadows through the branches of a large, old oak tree. Sketchy fingers coalesced on the far wall, and her heart pounded in her chest.

Was this a sign?

A welcome?

The shadows danced and then formed and appeared to be a finger pointing to her doom.

It was time.

Before Alden could push her, she stepped out into nothing.

Read The Haunting of Brynlee House now and always FREE on kindle unlimited

http://a-fwd.to/2UiiG7w

Never miss a book.

Subscribe to Caroline Clark's newsletter for new release announcements and occasional free content:

http://eepurl.com/cGdNvX

I am also a member of the haunted house collective.

Why not discover great new authors like me?

Enter your email address to get weekly newsletters of hot new haunted house books:

HauntedHouseBooks.info

About the Author

Caroline Clark is a British author who has always loved the macabre, the spooky, and anything that goes bump in the night.

She was brought up on stories from James Herbert, Shaun Hutson, Darcy Coates, and Ron Ripley. Even at school she was always living in her stories and was often asked to read them out in front of the class, though her teachers did not always appreciate her more sinister tales.

Now she spends her time researching haunted houses or imagining what must go on in them. These tales then get written up and become her books.

Caroline is married and lives in Yorkshire with her husband and their two white boxer dogs. Of course one of them is called Spooky.

You can contact Caroline via her Facebook page: https://www.facebook.com/CarolineClarkAuthor/

Or via her newsletter: http://eepurl.com/cGdNvX

She loves to hear from her readers.

Printed in Great Britain
by Amazon